DEATH AMONG THE NIGHTINGALES

Carlyle & West Mysteries
Book Four

David Field

SAPERE
BOOKS

Also in the Carlyle & West Mystery Series
Interviewing the Dead
Death Comes But Twice
Confronting the Invisible

DEATH AMONG THE NIGHTINGALES

Published by Sapere Books.

20 Windermere Drive, Leeds, England, LS17 7UZ,
United Kingdom

saperebooks.com

ISBN: 978-1-80055-157-2

1

18th June, 1895

Lieutenant-Colonel Hugh Charteris, Commanding Officer of 7 Company, Coldstream Guards, tapped the side of his wine glass with his dessert spoon and rose to his feet at the centre of the officer's mess dining table in the Waterloo barracks inside the Tower of London. It fell silent as the officers seated around the table reached for their own wine glasses ahead of being invited to rise and drink the toast that was imminent. All eyes except one man's drifted to the centre of the table and the commemorative plaque that the regiment had been awarded by the Duke of Wellington for the decisive role they had played in the defeat of Napoleon at Waterloo, as the Lieutenant-Colonel reminded them of why they were gathered.

'On this day, the 18th of June, exactly 80 years ago today, the Coldstream Guards of whom we are the proud regimental successors bravely held the gates of the Chateau of Hougoumont in what became known as the Battle of Waterloo. The Duke of Wellington himself was later to describe that glorious engagement as "the nearest-run thing you ever saw in your life" and in recognition of the heroism of our forebears in arms he presented the Coldstreamers with this memorial plaque on which is proudly displayed our regimental motto. And so I ask you to be upstanding, to raise your glasses and to proudly proclaim that we are indeed *"Nulli Secundus"* — second to none.'

He leaned forward and lifted the plaque from where it had been lying on the table in front of him. But before the officers by whom he was surrounded could rise to their feet, there was an ear-shattering explosion and the room became a maelstrom of flying glass and wood. Blood sprayed in fountains against the rear wall and uniformed men screamed as they succumbed to sickening injuries, before it all fell eerily silent.

Mess catering staff rushed in from the adjoining kitchens, then stopped dead at the horrible scene before them. The Lieutenant-Colonel was impaled on the rear wall by a large section of the former table that had shattered into shards, and what had been his lower limbs were reduced to bloodied stumps. All around the floor adjacent to his hideous corpse men were lying, some mercifully unconscious, some staring in disbelieving silence as the shock to their systems rendered them mute, while others began shrieking in agony as they vainly attempted to remove glass shards from facial lacerations.

Doctor James Carlyle had just returned home to Victoria Park Road, Hackney when a police coach rattled to a halt outside his front door and its uniformed occupant advised him breathlessly that he was urgently required back at the London Hospital, to which several Tower wagons bearing wounded Guards officers had delivered the victims of yet another Fenian bomb.

Carlyle was back at work within the hour, nudging his way through the chaos of the admission ward and briefly assessing each victim before issuing instructions to the limited number of nursing staff still on duty at seven o'clock on a Tuesday evening.

Ordering morphine for everyone lying on stretchers, and chloroform for a select few who were then conveyed on trolleys through the double set of heavy rubber doors that gave access to the operating room, he had, by the time he sank his weary and sickened body back into the coach home, amputated more limbs in three hours than he would expect to do in a year.

As he watched Bethnal Green slip past him in the darkness of Cambridge Road, he grimaced not only for the men who had been robbed of their pride as well as their mobility, but also for the group of so-called human beings who could inflict that sort of cowardly barbarity on another.

Life was also about to change for Detective Inspector John Jennings of Scotland Yard, who had been summoned to an urgent meeting with Assistant Commissioner Atkinson by means of a note awaiting him as he reported for duty the following morning. Atkinson wasted no time in offering Jennings a seat, but simply glared at him from behind his desk.

'You've heard of the latest outrage by these Fenian bastards?' he said.

'That business at the Tower last night? Could hardly not do, sir, given that every newspaper hawker between here and Islington's bellowing all about it at the top of their lungs.'

'I want you on the case immediately, Jennings. I've cleared it already with your chief superintendent.'

'But isn't that why we have an Irish Branch inside the Met, sir?'

'Indeed it is, for all the bloody use they seem to be. The Brotherhood are crowing their success all over the lower East End, and I'm advised that they're flying those damned green banners of theirs across the street from one tenement to another in Fern Street, down Bow way.'

'Poplar, actually,' Jennings corrected him. 'Fern Street and Rook Street are in Poplar, strictly speaking — the "Fenian Barracks", they call them.'

Atkinson smiled. 'Thank you for proving my point, John. You know that part of the lower East End better than anyone.'

'The Irish Branch must surely know more than I do about who's running the show,' Jennings countered. 'And as I'm sure you're aware, we lose more bobbies in that particular neck of the woods than the rest of London put together.'

'All the more reason why they need a seasoned officer at their head. I've made my decision and you will report to the chief inspector in Stepney today. You know what I'm looking for — a quick result and a few guilty Irishmen buckled and ready for the drop.'

'Yes, sir — but don't hold your breath. And don't expect me to hold it for you, because I'll be too busy holding my own.'

Matthew West assured his wife Adelaide for the tenth time that their daughter could be safely left under his supervision, if not his actual care. 'All I have to do is to make sure that Mrs Dunning changes her and feeds her as directed by you, with what was prepared by you and in accordance with that lengthy list of instructions that you've left her on the kitchen bench,' he said encouragingly.

Adelaide still looked reluctant to leave the house. 'Are you sure she can read?'

'Of *course* she can, or she'd make a very poor compiler of duty rosters for Sunday services. And given that she's had three children of her own, all of whom are now healthy and intelligent members of my Junior Bible Class, I think you can safely rely on her to look after a seven-month-old.'

Florence Kathleen Adelaide West had been born the previous October, following a confinement presided over by her grandfather Doctor James Carlyle and a delivery courtesy of the most experienced midwife in the London Hospital.

Nothing had been left to chance for the birth of the first child of the curate of St Dunstan's and his wife of less than three years who'd made such a name for herself while assisting her doctor father.

Among those who'd been impressed by her pioneering nursing efforts had been none other than Florence Nightingale, the legendary 'Lady of the Lamp', who'd made Adelaide an open offer to join her in the nursing school that she maintained inside St Thomas's Hospital whenever Adelaide felt ready.

After several soul-searching conversations with Matthew over the kitchen table, Adelaide had been persuaded that the day had come and that baby Florence would come to no harm if Adelaide finally took the plunge. A short letter to the lady herself had resulted in a swift reply confirming that 'Miss Nightingale' would be delighted to renew her acquaintance with Adelaide on the Monday following.

After several sleepless and conscience-ridden nights, Monday had arrived.

Adelaide mounted the steps to the entrance doors of St Thomas's Hospital and announced her arrival at the front desk to a harassed-looking clerk who invited her to take a seat on one of the benches. After the briefest of delays, a middle-aged nurse in a crisply starched uniform put Adelaide out of her mounting misery of self-doubt and invited her to follow her crackling skirts up two flights of stairs and down a corridor, at the end of which the sign on the glass door confirmed that they had reached their destination.

Florence Nightingale was slightly older looking than Adelaide remembered her as she levered herself out of her padded chair behind the massive mahogany desk in order to lean across it and offer a hand that Adelaide was not sure whether to shake or to kiss. Then she smiled kindly and nodded for Adelaide to take the seat in front of the desk. 'I was beginning to wonder if you'd forgotten me.'

'I could hardly do that,' Adelaide replied. 'I still can't believe that you think I might be of service to you.'

'Not me, my dear — medicine,' Florence corrected her. 'But first things first — how is your child?'

'Thriving, thank you. I hope you don't mind, but I had her christened Florence.'

'Quite the contrary — I'm flattered,' Florence said. 'It seems to be the fashion these days for girls to be named after their mothers, so I take it as a compliment that you chose my name.'

'I also named her after my own mother and then myself,' Adelaide admitted, slightly embarrassed. 'Her full name is Florence Kathleen Adelaide West.'

'If, one day, she's sent to a ladies' academy for her final tuition and it proves necessary to sew name labels into her clothing, you might regret that,' Florence all but chuckled, 'but now to business. Would you like some tea?'

'No thank you,' Adelaide replied demurely. 'To be perfectly frank with you, Miss Nightingale, I'm so nervous that I'd probably spill it all over my new costume.'

'Florence, please. As for being nervous, I feel sure you will be prepared, given the work you have done with your father.'

'It was he who saved people's lives,' Adelaide replied modestly.

Florence nodded. 'His was the medical knowledge, certainly, but nursing is just as much a profession as doctoring and the two work closely together. It's my philosophy that women should be able to follow professions just as much as men.'

'That's always been my philosophy too,' Adelaide replied. 'I've made it my life's work to campaign for women to be allowed to join professions such as the law and medicine.'

'And at a guess you've been entirely unsuccessful?' Florence asked with a wry smile.

Adelaide nodded. 'The men just form a defensive circle and blankly refuse to let women in.'

'All the more reason why women should make a profession of those areas of life that the men want nothing to do with, because they regard it as beneath them. Can you imagine a man agreeing to wipe up vomit and faeces? Holding a patient's hand while they're subjected to horrible processes? Washing patients who're not capable of doing it for themselves?'

'And yet those functions are just as important as knowing what medicines to administer, or how to amputate limbs.'

'Precisely. Which is why I've employed what little fame and influence I possess in order to make a profession out of nursing. You'll find that all the young ladies who graduate from my nursing school are precisely that — young ladies. Girls of breeding and education, who might otherwise have settled for being governesses or housekeepers. And I require them to *behave* like young ladies, too.' Florence reached out to lift a bulky document from the side of the table and handed it across to Adelaide. 'This is my "Code of Behaviour Manual" for all "Nightingale Nurses", as they've become known. Your task will be to ensure that it's complied with at all times and in all those hospitals to which my nurses are despatched.'

Adelaide opened it and ran her eyes down it briefly. Her eyebrows rose slightly as she read some of the strictures, then she smiled. 'How do the nurses react to all these rules?'

'They obey them,' came the slightly starchy reply. 'Particularly those that relate to not forming any personal relationships with their patients. Doctors don't do it and neither, so far as I'm aware, do the men in other professions, and so it's in keeping with the professional image that I wish nurses to develop that they behave likewise. The patients can too easily regard their nurses as angels of mercy or substitute mothers, and it's not a healthy image for them to foster. Regardless of how intimate their contact with a patient has to be — and *particularly* if they're men and the procedure is one of extreme intimacy — it's imperative that a professional distance is maintained.'

Adelaide thought for a moment before replying as tactfully as she could. 'I could perceive a situation in which a woman trains as a nurse *precisely* in order to find a husband, if that's not too indelicate an observation to make.'

'Indeed it's not, and you're quite right that some of them in the past have joined my nursing classes for precisely that reason. They normally only last a month or so, until the romance is knocked out them by a succession of bed-pan duties, or the need to dress amputation stubs. But a few still find themselves drawn to a man whose hand they've been holding for weeks, through the most emotional and intimate procedures. It will be your task to ensure that they maintain their professionalism and I will be sending you out to reinforce my mission.'

'Sending me out where, exactly?' Adelaide asked with a look of concern. 'My young daughter's needs must be given priority, so I wouldn't wish to be sent too far away for any great length of time.'

'Does your husband not assist? Or is he one of those men whose only contribution to families is to be present when they are conceived?'

'No, please don't get the wrong impression,' Adelaide hastened to explain. 'He's wonderful — so helpful and attentive, and he dotes on our daughter. It's just that he's, well — not very practical, let's say. But one of the parish women has been employed to ensure that Florence gets fed, changed and nursed when appropriate. I think she may be cutting another tooth at present and she's apt to cry a lot.'

'Your husband is the curate of St Dunstan's, is he not, and he has church duties to fulfil?'

'Yes, that's right, and the vicar is beginning to feel his age, so Matthew's being required to shoulder more and more of the parish duties.'

'While you have to pay a woman to look after your child?'

'Yes, but that's not a problem, since … well, to be perfectly frank with you I'm in the fortunate position of enjoying an independent income, thanks to my father and his wise guidance in the matter of investments. We don't even rely on Matthew's stipend, which is perhaps as well, since it's so meagre.'

'I will obviously be paying you a small salary in return for your supervision of my nurses in the matter of their professionalism,' Florence said. 'It should at least cover the cost of your child's day nurse, but little more, so perhaps it's as well that you have the means to live comfortably while assisting me. The least I can do is to ensure that your journeys from home are kept to a minimum, particularly while your child is still in her infancy.'

'So how do you organise the deployment of your nurses?' Adelaide asked.

Florence glowed with pride as she sat back and supplied the answer. 'I am very fortunate that Nightingale Nurses are in high demand throughout the realm. There are very few hospitals left across the country that do not have a team of them. And I make it a term of their engagement that they are to be kept in the same team that leaves from here at the end of their training. Apart from the natural friendships that they've already formed during the rigorous demands of that training, it's better for them that they remain in their teams, to provide ongoing support for each other and benefit from such arrangements as sharing lodgings, mutually maintaining their professionalism and so on. You will be required to visit these teams periodically and represent me. I hope that they will come to dread your visits, in the sense that they will regard them as tantamount to visits from me, enforcing the professionalism with the same rigour that I would do.'

'I'm very conscious of the honour that you're paying me and the trust that you're prepared to invest in my work,' Adelaide replied nervously.

'Then see that you live up to it,' Florence replied with a smile. 'And your first visitation will not require you to venture far from home, or indeed from family.' When Adelaide looked puzzled, Florence added, 'Your father is the senior surgeon at the London Hospital, is he not?'

'Yes.'

'You will of course be aware of that dreadful explosion at the Tower Barracks a week or so ago?'

'Of course.'

'Well, your father commandeered an entire ward of the hospital for those victims who survived it, then sent a request for me to send him nurses trained to deal with the worst possible cases. As you are aware, I first made my name tending to the needs of those who had been injured in the Crimea, and he thought it likely that I would have trained my nurses for just such a challenge — nursing military casualties. And of course I had. Two days ago I sent a group of eight of my most recent graduates to him, to staff the additional male surgical ward that he's established for those who were dragged out of the horror and confusion of that wicked bomb attack. I require you to enquire as to their welfare. And, of course, to ensure that they're adhering strictly to my professional code of behaviour. No doubt you welcome the chance to work alongside your father once again, so your return to work could not have been more aptly timed. Welcome to your new profession, Adelaide.'

2

'I hope you weren't too inconvenienced,' Reverend Joseph Mulholland said to his curate, Matthew West, as they were allowed through the police cordon that had been in place for over a week by a bored-looking constable who was counting the minutes until his relief arrived. 'Only it's always been one of the ecclesiastical duties of the incumbent of St. Dunstan's to minister to the Tower Guards. The arrangement goes so far back into the past, to the days when it was the only parish church for the whole of the East End, that no-one seems to have ever questioned it since. They still trot out the Bishop for formal occasions when Her Majesty puts in an appearance, but the day-to-day stuff falls to us, and this time I'm really going to need you along with me to cope with all the unrequited grief.'

'Don't the individual regiments have their own padres?' Matthew asked. 'I recall meeting one of them a few years ago.'

Mulholland nodded. 'Yes, they do, and the Coldstreamers are no different, apparently. But he's ducking this one since the Company that copped the bomb were on Tower duty at the time. Can't say I blame him, but you'll need to brace yourself to comfort a sad line of broken-hearted widows, I'm afraid. Good of you to agree to accompany me.'

'I wouldn't want to tackle it on my own,' Matthew admitted, 'so I don't see why you should have to. And at least you'll be conducting the Memorial Service on your own.'

The largely ceremonial guards on either side of the main entrance to the imposing Waterloo Barracks ignored them and continued to stare straight ahead into the middle distance. It was a uniformed captain who opened the doors from the inside as he saw the two clergymen approaching, identifiable by their dog collars. He smiled invitingly as he held the double doors open for them to enter.

'Thank you for coming along, gentlemen. I'm Captain Murray, Adjutant to the Colonel in Chief of the Regiment. He's the top man around here, obviously, and he'll be doing the honours, since we lost the Lieutenant-Colonel in the big bang. It's this way.'

He led them into the assembly hall, full to capacity with men in full Mess uniform, women dressed in funereal black and restless but sad children sitting bolt upright on chairs too big for them. Matthew took a seat to the side and watched as Joseph Mulholland worked his way dutifully through a Memorial Service to the accompaniment of the occasional strangled sob from a widow, or a hushed enquiry from a small child as to what was taking place and why they couldn't go outside to play. The final Blessing was followed by a bugler rendering a slightly wavering 'Last Post' and a piper in full Highland regalia who played the platform party out of the hall to the haunting pibroch of 'Flowers of the Forest'.

Matthew caught up with his superior in the smaller room to the side where tea and sandwiches were being served and Mulholland was being regaled with a history of the Coldstreamers by its commanding officer. The look on the vicar's face could not have been more expressive of someone in need of rescue, and Matthew dutifully walked over to be introduced.

'I was just saying to the padre here that if we could only get five minutes alone with the cowards who planted that bomb, we'd make drum skins out of their arses,' the colonel thundered for the second time.

'And I was just reminding him of Christ's admonition that "To one who strikes you on the cheek, offer the other also",' Mulholland added.

'Fat chance!' the colonel blustered. 'You're talking to a fighting man at the head of the finest regiment in the British Army, remember. If Wellington had turned his cheek to Napoleon, we'd all be speaking French now, dammit!'

'How have the families been bearing up?' Matthew asked diplomatically in an effort to change the subject.

'No idea,' the colonel replied. 'Isn't that why you're here? We've set aside a couple of rooms alongside the Sergeants' Mess, by the way, and you can dispense your tea and sympathy in there. Well, the sympathy, anyway. Good job there's two of you, because there are several widows and a handful of wives whose husbands will be returning with bits missing. Anyway, must push on — lots of folk to gladhand and all that.'

Matthew's first encounter was with a Mrs Kelly, widow of Captain Giles Kelly.

'We did our best for many years to have children,' she said. 'Even when Giles was managing that family farm outside Tadcaster and I was the local schoolteacher. Then he joined the regiment and we had many months at a time apart from each other, so the chances of my falling pregnant were reduced. We were so happy when we discovered that I was expecting Luke. He'll be two next year, and somebody has to tell him that he doesn't have a father. Would you be good enough to do that for me, please?'

Her face crumpled and the tears came in shudders and gulps. Matthew reached out for her hands, taking each of hers in each of his. She eventually became aware of the silent gesture and threw his consoling hands off as if they were live snakes, her face a mask of angry revulsion.

'Don't pretend to comfort me! Call yourself a man of God? Where was God when Giles was taken from me? Where was your precious Jesus when my man's legs were blown clean off? Now you have the nerve to come in here and pretend that you care? You're a hypocrite and I can't stand the sight of you!'

She rose from her chair and rushed out of the room. Matthew was too shocked to try to restrain her.

Another solemn face appeared in the doorway, and Matthew indicated the recently vacated seat with a trembling hand. This next lady was much more composed and looked Matthew up and down appraisingly as she took the seat across the table and introduced herself as Ursula Charteris.

'My husband Hugh was the Lieutenant-Colonel in command of the Seventh Company. You must forgive Emily Kelly; she's taken the loss of her husband very deeply.'

'As have you all,' Matthew suggested, to be met with raised eyebrows.

'Really? You think that? Have you the remotest idea what it's like to be married to a man who treats you like one of his batmen, always on hand to fawn and scrape and fulfil his every command? And I mean *every* command, young man, although in deference to your calling I won't go into graphic detail. Believe me, retirement to Brighton on a generous widow's pension will be a blessed relief, and I only popped into this dreary room because there'd be gossip of quite the wrong sort if I didn't. Just wave your hand in blessing or something and let me out of here.'

Matthew did as requested, shocked to his very core, and was almost relieved to see that his next encounter would be with a lady whose defeated look suggested that she was in mourning. He invited her to take the seat opposite his at the table and opted to initiate the conversation.

'Be assured that God sees your grief and will carry you through this Vale of Sorrow. Just offer your sufferings up to Him and His loving arms will enfold you.'

'Will they also pay my husband's debts?' the lady asked.

'He died indebted?' Matthew responded. 'I'm no lawyer, but I'm led to believe that one's debts die with one.'

'He's not dead,' the lady all but spat. 'Just blinded, which hopefully means that he won't be able to see the cards anymore. And since he won't be a soldier either, he won't have any money to fritter away around the table inside that dreadful whorehouse where he spent so many of his nights. As to how we'll feed the three children, well, there's always one option available to a lady who's already lost her pride but not her looks, is there not?'

Matthew's jaw dropped and he sought frantically for something to say.

She smiled across at him sympathetically as she broke the stunned silence. 'You must forgive me if my bitterness sometimes does the talking for me. I know I should be crying all over you and seeking God's intervention to save Gerard's life, but to be perfectly honest I don't know if he's really worth it. I'll have his mouth to feed now, as well as mine and our children's, because I don't suppose that there's much call for the services of a blinded ex-soldier.'

'If you give me his name, I could always ask around my Stepney parish,' Matthew offered. 'I know that we have a Poor Relief Fund, and from time to time we get requests for men to work on things such as road digging in order to supply employment to the indigent.'

'For what it's worth, my name's Mary Logan and my husband is Captain Gerard Logan, Adjutant to the former Lieutenant-Colonel. He was blinded in the blast.'

Two hours and several allegedly grieving Army wives and widows later, Matthew was glad to make his way back up Tower Hill alongside Joseph Mulholland, whose afternoon had been no more uplifting than Matthew's. They sank back into the padded seats of the coach that was always available to the vicar from a parishioner anxious to make it through the Pearly Gates with his sins forgiven, and Matthew sighed noisily.

'There are days when I regret having given up street preaching, and this has been one of them. At least those to whom I ministered then led uncomplicated lives. Now to learn what Florrie's been up to today in my absence.'

Adelaide West crept surreptitiously through the double swing doors into 'The Tower Ward', as it had been renamed and stood silently just inside, hoping not to be noticed in the pool of gloom beyond the range of the gas lamps that lined the walls. Three nurses were passing silently between the eight beds on the ward, only six of which were currently occupied, while a fourth sat at a centre desk, receiving reports from the other three and transferring their contents into a 'Ward Report' book. At least they looked the part, with their dark blue floor-length gowns and their stiffly starched white aprons and matching bonnets. As they moved gracefully between beds, all that could be heard was the squeak of the soft soles of their uniform shoes against the linoleum, and Adelaide smiled to herself as she stepped into the first pool of light.

The nurse at the centre table looked up with a start and called out, 'No visitors at this hour! Those are the regulations.'

'And I'm delighted to note that you enforce them,' Adelaide replied as she walked towards the centre desk. 'Perhaps I could also check that your Ward Report is up to date. It's now shortly after ten in the evening, so it should be completed up to at least nine.'

'Who are you to be asking to see the Ward Report?' the nurse at the desk demanded as she hunched defensively over the book in front of her.

Adelaide walked to the other side of the desk, sat down and opened her bag to extract a bound notebook. 'I'm Adelaide West, and I believe that Miss Nightingale may have warned you to expect me.'

'You work with her?' came the enquiry from behind the desk as the other nurses moved towards it.

'With her and *for* her, in a manner of speaking. My official title is "Placement Supervisor", and I'm here to ensure that you are adhering to the Pledge that you all signed and are carrying out your duties in accordance with the protocols that were instilled in you along with your nursing training. I should perhaps begin with your names.'

'I'm Edith Crawford,' the girl at the desk replied with a smile. 'The one with the fair hair and freckles is my cousin Lily Becket.'

'I'm Doris Mooney,' announced a tall, thin woman with red hair, while the final one of the four introduced herself as Mary Brennan with an open, generous smile in a broad, ruddy face that might have belonged on a farmer's wife.

Adelaide made a note of their names, then asked, 'You're the night duty team?'

'That's right,' Edith Crawford confirmed. 'We're here from six in the evening until six tomorrow morning, then the other four take over from us. They're Ellen Tring, Annie Bestwood, Ethel Beamish and Alice Tremayne.'

Completing her note of the names, Adelaide looked to her right and left, towards the silent beds. 'Your patients are all survivors of that terrible bomb at the Tower, I understand. Could someone give me a swift note of their names, their injuries and their treatment regimens?'

Once again it was Edith Crawford who seemed to take the natural lead, and Adelaide made a mental note that she appeared to have leadership potential, should there be an occasion to appoint a Matron directly over the Nightingale Nurses.

'There are six patients in all, as you can see, three on each side of the ward. The beds are numbered from the entrance down, so that the first occupied bed on the left as you look back towards the door is Bed Two. It currently contains Captain John Sweeney, whose chest injuries may yet prove fatal.' She'd lowered her voice to advise Adelaide of this, as if fearful that the man in question might overhear. 'Next to him, in Bed Three, is Major Tom Curran, who lost his right arm to amputation. He's in considerable pain and requires the most morphine, although otherwise he's in good spirits and even chats with the nurses while they change his dressings. A very brave man, and were we allowed to get emotional, we'd all be in floods of tears at his bravery.'

'Bed Four?' Adelaide prompted her, and the information was supplied as briefly and efficiently as for the others.

'That's Captain Gerard Logan, with flash burns to his face and damage to his eyes. Doctor Carlyle instructed that his eyes be kept bandaged at all times, and none of us has any idea if he'll ever see again.' Edith's voice had fallen to almost a whisper by this point, and Adelaide turned to look up the right hand side of the ward.

'Bed Six?' she asked, and the answer was as readily forthcoming as the others.

'Lieutenant Peter Hargraves, minus his left leg below the knee. Likewise Captain James Owen in Bed Seven, who also lost his left hand as well as his left foot. Finally, the youngest of them, Captain Michael Collington, peppered with broken glass during the explosion, more of which we keep discovering every time we bathe him — very carefully, of course.'

'And these are *all* your patients?' Adelaide asked, a little puzzled. 'If so, then you have a patient allocation far lower than normal — better than two to one.'

'That was Matron Beswick's instruction,' Edith explained, 'and she told us that it came from Doctor Carlyle himself. The injuries are severe and the patients are deserving of the highest standards of care — that's what we were told.'

'Why are the other two beds empty?' Adelaide persevered. 'Are these all the casualties from the Tower explosion?'

'All that are left,' Edith replied sadly. 'There *were* two more, but they died of their injuries. And the ones who remain are so much in need of constant care that none of us were transferred to other duties.'

'Do you intend to maintain the same duty allocations from week to week, so that you four are on permanent night duties, with no opportunities for lives of your own?'

'These patients have only been here for the past two weeks,' Edith reminded her, 'and we were sent by Miss Nightingale with the specific mission to take care of them. We were the ones who divided ourselves into two groups of four, and should any of us feel the need for change, then it will be the simplest thing to organise, since together we rent rooms in a house in Whitechapel where we all live and share the rental and other costs. We agreed that we'd change the duty hours after the first month, so in two weeks' time if you come into the ward at this time of the evening you'll find Ellen, Annie, Ethel and Alice on duty.'

Adelaide smiled. 'Well, you seem to have matters well organised, and I can't pretend to comment on the standard of nursing. I'll call in tomorrow morning and speak to the other four, but I'm sure there'll be no problem.'

As Adelaide left for home she was full of admiration for the dedication and professionalism of these young women. After all, they were abandoning all immediate prospect of marriage and childbirth. Then as she boarded the horse bus she smiled at her own short memory; four years ago she would have laughed out loud at the suggestion that she'd find a man and get herself married and then pregnant. But that was before she met Matthew West.

3

'Any tea on the go?' Inspector Jennings enquired as he pushed open the door and looked across at James Carlyle, who was making the opening incision into the corpse of a vagrant, whose facial lesions were suggestive of a pestilence.

Carlyle looked up with a mild frown. 'This is a hospital mortuary, not a coffee house. This is my mortuary assistant, Martin Preedy. Martin, allow me to introduce Inspector John Jennings of Scotland Yard, who seems to regard this medical facility as some sort of cafeteria and only shows up when he wants something.'

Jennings nodded towards the gangly youth who was mixing substances over a low gas flame on the bench to the side of the dissection table, then turned back to Carlyle. 'I always got a warmer welcome when your daughter was here to improve your social skills.'

'I'm sure that you're not here to comment on Adelaide's absence. Why precisely are you here?'

'I want your approval to visit those poor buggers who got themselves blown up by Fenians in the Tower.'

'The Guards officers?' Carlyle asked. 'Out of the question.'

'This is obviously not only a multiple murder enquiry, but also a matter of considerable national urgency,' Jennings reminded him. 'We need to nail those responsible and quickly. I can't do that without working out how the bomb was sneaked into there in the first place and in particular where it was placed. I had hoped that the walking wounded could give me a clue to that and could perhaps further advise me of any suspicious movements just before the explosion.'

'They are *far* from being "walking" wounded, as you describe them,' Carlyle sniffed as he gave up the attempt at dissection and threw the scalpel into the instrument tray with a loud clatter. 'They are lying prone with serious injuries, some of them minus limbs and all of them separated from physical agony only by dedicated nursing and the liberal application of morphine. That same morphine tends to addle their thought processes, so even were I to grant you permission to talk to them, they'd be likely to yield only gibberish. If it comes to that, are you not able to pinpoint the precise location of the bomb by your own scientific processes?'

Jennings sighed. 'You have obviously not visited the site of the explosion. It's a total mess, a rubbish pile of wood, glass, cutlery and bloodied remains. Or at least, it was. All we have left after cleaning it up is a big hole in the wooden floor.'

'Far be it from me to perform your work for you, but does that not suggest that the bomb was located on that portion of the floor that is now a memory?'

'You employ your skills and I'll apply mine,' Jennings retorted tartly. 'The nature of an explosive device is such that it blows outwards in all directions. For all I know, the bomb was strapped to the underside of the table and the hole was caused by a downward percussive force.'

'However, that doesn't rule out the possibility that it was lying on the floor, which would be consistent with the injuries that I saw on the men being brought into the hospital, all of which were suggestive of a destructive force driving upwards and outwards.'

'So I can't go onto the ward and speak to the men themselves?' Jennings countered. 'There's a very officious "Nurse Tring" down there who's adamant that I don't get to even wave to the poor buggers without your approval, hence my presence here this morning.'

'I'm delighted to learn that Miss Nightingale's graduates are so dedicated to their patients' health. It will also please Adelaide, who's in charge of them in a manner of speaking. And you know Adelaide well enough not to try to go behind her back. However, I may be able to assist in two other ways.'

'Go on?'

'If you can provide me with a diagram of who was seated where at the dinner table when the bomb went off, it might be possible to determine the point of explosion from the nature and location of their injuries.'

'I'm sure I can do that. What's the second thing you can do for me?'

'Supply you with a mug of tea. I could also manage one, since I'm clearly not going to be allowed to continue with this post-mortem. Martin, please put some water on to boil, if you'd be so obliging.'

'Do you think any of those poor men might benefit from a visit from a clergyman?' Matthew asked Adelaide.

'I doubt it, at present,' she replied. 'They're up to their eyeballs in morphine and not making any sort of rational sense at the moment. Then again, since religion falls into the same category, who knows?'

Matthew sighed. 'I really chose the wrong profession from your perspective, didn't I?'

'No,' she replied quietly as she snuggled closer to him under the bed covers, 'since it made you the man you are. The man I love. And it's what you wanted to do, so it makes you happy.'

'*You* make me happy,' Matthew assured her as he kissed the top of her head. 'It's just that I spent a miserable afternoon speaking to the widows and wives of the men who were caught up in that cowardly Fenian bomb. I got the shock of my life when I realised how little love there was in those marriages. Do *all* marriages finish up like that? Or is it the case that God has forsaken them because their lives are filled with warfare and aggression?'

'It's awful, I know,' Adelaide murmured. 'Some of those poor wretches have never yet been visited by their wives, did you know? Are they too fearful of confronting the injuries that their men have suffered, some of them crippled for life? Or do they genuinely not care for them?'

'How did it go with the nurses?' Matthew asked, rather than fumbling for a direct answer to her question.

'I think they accepted why I was there and they're doing a magnificent job. But I feel sorry for them, in another sense. They've got no lives of their own outside nursing.'

'Perhaps nursing *is* their life.'

'Perhaps. That's certainly true for Florence, I believe. I wonder if she ever had a gentleman friend.'

'Don't enquire too closely, or another illusion might be shattered,' Matthew counselled her. 'For all you know, she had a mad affair behind the scenes with some Army Colonel out in the Crimea.'

Adelaide giggled. 'I really can't imagine her hoisting her crinoline and bending over a gunpowder barrel. She's far too ladylike and proper for anything like that.'

Just then they heard a faint whimper from the adjoining room and waited with bated breath for the full-throated wail that they knew would follow.

'Whose turn is it?' Matthew asked with resignation.

'Yours, dearest. I have to be at the hospital early in the morning.'

Adelaide was sitting at the table in the centre of the Tower Ward, chatting to Ellen Tring, when the double doors were thrown open and Matron Beswick bustled in, followed by a very familiar figure.

'Doctor Carlyle is here for his morning round, so look lively!' Matron ordered everyone, before piercing Adelaide with a glare. 'And who might *you* be?' she demanded.

Carlyle smiled as he waved Adelaide over to his side. 'I believe this lady to be Mrs West, who is here representing Miss Nightingale. Since her nurses are doing such a fine job for us here, it's perhaps only fitting that she accompanies me round the beds while you perhaps go about your duties elsewhere, Matron.'

Ellen Tring suppressed a snigger as she heard the formidable Matron Beswick put in her place. Adelaide turned to her and whispered, 'You know them better than I, Ellen, so please come with me.'

Carlyle began with Bed Two, where Ellen took up a position down one side and Adelaide on the other, while Carlyle looked down from in front.

'Captain Sweeney, Doctor,' Ellen told him. 'Many chest injuries, as you no doubt recall, but he seems to be making steady progress and there's no sign of any wound infection. We're administering iodine every four hours.'

'I'm sorry for you,' Carlyle muttered to the patient. 'They tell me that it stings something fierce, but fortunately I've never needed it.'

'So long as it makes me better,' the captain grimaced back. 'When can I go home?'

Carlyle made a few pencilled notes on the paper that he had attached to a clipboard. 'Give it another week or so, then we'll consider discharging you.'

'A *week*?' Sweeney protested. 'I was hoping to take a few days of leave down in Kent before the Company's deployed to Aldershot. My girl lives in Broadstairs.'

'So she's not been able to visit you?'

'No. I wrote to her that I'd be coming down to see her in the first week of July, but she doesn't know I'm in hospital.'

Carlyle fixed Adelaide with a smile. 'Since your husband is a clergyman, perhaps he might wish to write to the young lady in question, on behalf of this brave officer? Apart from anything else, if she's heard about the bomb outrage and she knows that her young man was on duty at the Tower at the time, she's probably frantic with worry.'

'I'll see that he does, Doctor,' Adelaide replied warmly.

Captain Sweeney thanked them both profusely and the party of three moved down to the next bed.

'This is Major Curran,' Ellen told Carlyle. 'You amputated his right arm, but he's been complaining of late that he can still feel pain in the missing limb. We're administering as much morphine as is consistent with the appropriate dosage, but we find that we can distract him by sitting and chatting with him during his more lucid moments.'

Carlyle nodded. 'The pains from the missing arm are quite normal, I'm afraid. He appears to be asleep at the moment — has he recently had morphine?'

'Just before you came on your ward round,' Ellen confirmed. 'I'm sorry if you wanted him awake for your visit.'

'No, far from it,' Carlyle reassured her. 'Just don't overdo the morphine, that's all.'

They moved to Bed Three and the man who was lying there had his face almost completely obscured by bandages.

'Captain Logan,' Ellen announced loudly and clearly, 'Doctor Carlyle's here to see you.'

'Pardon me if I don't get up and shake your hand,' Logan replied.

Carlyle grinned. 'You can probably do that in a few more days. How are the burns?'

'Painful, thank you for enquiring,' Logan muttered bitterly. 'But what'll be happening in next few days, exactly?'

'The bandages will be coming off, then we'll get to know how your eyes have fared through all this.'

'Whether or not I'll be blind for the rest of my life, you mean? Now *there's* something to look forward to.'

'You haven't lost your fighting spirit, anyway,' Carlyle replied as he motioned for Ellen and Adelaide to walk back to the desk with him. Once they reached it, Carlyle lowered his voice to issue an instruction. 'I'll supply Mrs West here with some powder that is to be mixed in with tea, milk, or whatever liquid is administered to Captain Logan. It's to be used sparingly, but it should serve to lift his spirits. He's in danger of a nervous collapse, so far as I can deduce, and the powder will help to keep him cheerful and positive.'

'St John's Wort?' Adelaide asked without thinking.

Carlyle nodded. 'St John's Wort, indeed. As you have no doubt deduced for yourself, Nurse,' he said to Ellen, 'Mrs West has a clear memory of the days when she worked as my mortuary assistant and acquired a good deal of pharmacological knowledge. Now let's see the other patients.'

Carlyle had been noting down all the injuries as he passed between the patient beds, and by the time that he declared himself ready to leave he had several pages of scribbled notes. Nurse Annie Bestwood was despatched to find Matron Beswick and advise her that Doctor Carlyle was ready to visit the next ward. Adelaide took the seat on the other side of the desk from Ellen Tring while Carlyle stood by the ward doors, awaiting his escort and reading his notes.

'Is it true that you used to work for Doctor Carlyle?' Ellen whispered, clearly impressed.

Adelaide nodded. 'Almost seven years altogether,' she replied. 'He's a remarkable doctor, although not always conventional in his approach, as you will have deduced from his prescription of St John's Wort. But if the patient complains of nausea, stop administering it immediately. Likewise if the patient should require morphine.'

'You almost sound like a doctor yourself,' Ellen said admiringly.

Adelaide smiled. 'There were times I felt like one, believe me, such was Doctor Carlyle's encouragement of me to learn all I could under his guidance.'

Carlyle looked up from the latest edition of *The Lancet* as the mortuary door opened and Inspector Jennings walked in. 'We must train you to knock, Inspector. Or are you so accustomed to kicking in doors without invitation that you never think to knock anymore?'

'Never mind the social conventions,' Jennings growled. 'I need your conclusion regarding where that bomb was placed, since I've got myself a suspect.'

'Really? Who might that be?'

'A man called Padraig Murphy, who works in the kitchens attached to the Officers' Mess in Waterloo Barracks.'

'And does he have a history of violence or subversion?'

'No, but he has an Irish name and he would have had access to the dining table while the officers were having pre-dinner drinks at the bar next door.'

'I have a Scots name,' Carlyle observed with a frown. 'Does that make me a covert Jacobite?'

'Of course not,' Jennings snapped, 'but if you can tell me that the bomb was probably strapped to the underside of the table, then that would give me a good reason to arrest Murphy on suspicion.'

Carlyle sighed. 'I seem destined to disappoint you yet again, Inspector, so the least I can do is offer you some tea. Have you brought along that seating plan you promised me?'

A few minutes later, Carlyle could only confuse matters for his visitor as he studied the table plan and pencilled a few notes on it before handing it across the bench and inviting Jennings to examine it for himself.

'As you can probably work out without my assistance, it's almost certain that the explosive was under the table, most probably on the floor and somewhere in the centre.'

'That may be obvious to you,' Jennings grumbled, 'but you'll need to explain it to me.'

'I must admit,' Carlyle conceded, 'that it's easier when you consider the injuries that each victim suffered, which I noted in pencil alongside their names. But those injuries form a distinctive, and very revealing, pattern.'

'Go on,' Jennings invited him without any discernible enthusiasm, and Carlyle duly obliged.

'We begin at the centre of the table and the Lieutenant-Colonel, who died swiftly and horribly when he caught the full blast of a heavy table blown to shards, clearly from underneath it somewhere. The impact was such that it shredded the table *before* it hit him, whereas had the explosive been strapped to the underside of the table the entire table would have lifted and probably removed his head in the process. This suggests to me that the explosive was lying on the floor under the table and that is consistent with the large shard that impaled him on the wall behind.'

'I suppose I have to accept that,' Jennings grumbled, 'but it weakens my case against Murphy.'

'Not necessarily, since he would have been able to place it on the floor even more quickly than taping it to the underside of the table. Any idea of how it was detonated, by the way?'

'Not really,' Jennings admitted. 'We found a few bits of burned wire, so it appears to have been connected to something, but God knows what, at this stage.'

'Anyway,' Carlyle continued, 'the remaining casualties suggest that the bomb was almost immediately in front of the Lieutenant-Colonel's feet — perhaps touching his toes.'

'How do you work that out?'

'Well, look at the spread of the injuries. The men on either side of the Lieutenant-Colonel, Major Kelly to his immediate right and Captain Mullens on his left, were killed outright and their bodies were retrieved in various instalments. Second from the right of Kelly was Hargraves and he survived minus his left leg below the knee, which again suggests an impact from below and to his left. Second from the left of Mullens was Captain Sweeney, who suffered chest injuries only, suggesting that the percussive effect by that point down the table was more upward than outward. This hypothesis is borne out by the injuries to Major Curran, seated between Mullens and Sweeney, who lost his right arm but nothing else. The further down that table they were sitting, to judge by the injuries, the less direct the impact. This is all suggestive of an upward percussive blow, which when it reached the far end of the table was mainly delivering a great deal of flying glass from the wine glasses and decanter.'

'So the ones down the end of the table on each side had a lucky escape?' Jennings conjectured.

Carlyle shrugged. 'In the case of Captain Collington on the far left, certainly. He was peppered with broken glass and may well prove to be the first to be discharged from hospital. That leaves a puzzle at the far right hand end of the table as we look at your seating plan.'

'Captain Logan?'

'The very same. No broken or severed limbs, but extensive flash burns to the face, including his eyes, the use of which may well be lost to him.'

'Surely there's a flash from any explosive?'

'There certainly is, if you're at eye level with it. But if it was under the table when it went off, why did Logan cop the flash burns? Or, more to the point, *how*?'

'None of that is immediately important, surely?' Jennings argued.

Carlyle raised his eyebrows. 'It might be — who can tell, at this stage?'

'You make it sound as if this is going to take a long time, whereas all I need to do is arrest Murphy and interrogate him regarding his Irish associations.'

'Even in *this* county, being Irish hasn't yet become an offence,' Carlyle reminded him. 'You're going to need more than that.'

'That's what interrogations are for,' Jennings replied ominously. 'Thank you for your assistance — not that I think it takes us much further. Even if, as you say, the explosive was simply laid on the floor, that doesn't absolve Murphy. As you yourself pointed out, it just made it easier for him.'

'And easier for anyone else,' Carlyle reminded him. 'You should be asking more questions of the Guards officers around the table, when that's possible.'

'And I will, once you patch them up and release them.'

'So, have you got the address of this young lady from Broadstairs?' Matthew asked Adelaide over the tea table.

Adelaide reached down to the bag lying at her feet, extracted the piece of paper and laid it down in front of him. 'Try not to cause her any alarm,' she said.

'I think I can help to soothe her troubles. Now, do you want to go and admire Florrie's second tooth?'

'Not if it'll wake her up again. And stop calling her "Florrie".'

'Everyone else will, and "Florence" sounds so formal and pompous for a cute little bundle like her.'

'Well, your cute little bundle will need feeding when she does wake up, and I vote for Daddy to do the feeding.'

'I'm getting used to it lately. How long will you be required to visit the hospital every day?'

'Until the Tower Ward empties and the Nightingale Nurses are dispersed from their current duties and spread around other wards. We just have to hope that the next hospital I'm sent to isn't in Liverpool or somewhere, although one day it'll come to that.'

'Let me know when and if your wounded patients are allowed home and I'll establish a series of visits,' Matthew offered.

They both grimaced as the wail became audible from somewhere up above them.

'Your first visit will be upstairs, I believe,' Adelaide said. 'But you won't be making it alone. After being surrounded by all this pain and suffering, I need a moment of gentleness and peace. And it's time that our daughter was reminded that she has a mother, as well as a father who can't even get her name right.'

4

A week later Matthew and Adelaide stood, craning their necks over those in front of them at the arrival gate of the London, Chatham and Dover line service from Broadstairs, watching the guard's van approaching the buffers cautiously as the puffing engine at the far end of the train eased the five passenger carriages slowly down the platform.

The carriage doors opened and the passengers began to make their way to the gate, to be met and hugged by waiting family and friends. The lady they were awaiting duly appeared and there was no mistaking the feathered blue bonnet that she'd promised to wear in order to be easily recognised.

'Lila Drake?' Adelaide asked as the lady reached them through the heaving crowd and Matthew leaned forward to take her travelling bag.

Lila nodded enthusiastically as she replied, 'You must be Reverend and Mrs West — it's *so* good of you to go to all this trouble just for John and myself. How is he, do you know? Is he badly injured?'

'No, rest assured,' Adelaide replied. 'His chest injuries were quite severe at the time, but that was over two weeks ago now and he's making a very encouraging recovery, under the care of the finest team of nurses in London.'

'I understand that you're one of them,' Lila said. 'I really can't thank you enough for all your efforts. John's the most important person in my life, after my elderly parents, and we plan on getting married later this year. Will he have to leave the Army, do you think?'

'I'm not one of his nurses, so I can't take any of the credit for the wonderful treatment that your young man's been receiving, although it was my father who had to remove quite a bit of glass and wood from wounds to his chest. As I said, he's making splendid progress now, but whether or not he'll be able to resume his Army career will obviously be a decision for the Army itself. Now, shall we have a cup of tea in the cafeteria here before we go to the hospital to see him, or do you wish to go first to wherever you're staying? We can always give you a bed for the night if you haven't fixed up anywhere yet.'

'That's very kind of you, but I have a sister who lives in Finchley and I always stay with her when I'm in London. That's how John and I met — at a dance organised by her church group for Coldstream Guards officers returning from Egypt. However, a cup of tea would be most welcome, since I always find that the steam and soot from trains leaves me with quite a dry throat.'

After a pot of tea and a series of bus trips through the bustling metropolis, they alighted at the London Hospital and escorted Lila up the main staircase to the Tower Ward on the first floor. Adelaide entered the ward first, to ensure that Captain Sweeney was in a fit state to receive a visitor and not lost in some morphia-induced slumber. Then she led a nervous Lila Drake into the ward and retreated diplomatically while the two lovers exchanged cries of delight, kisses, tears and loving endearments.

'Thank you *so* much, dear lady!' John Sweeney called out to Adelaide as she walked back into the ward accompanied by Matthew and made her way towards the empty desk in the centre of the room. She looked down with a frown at the closed Ward Report Book, opened it at the current page and snorted faintly as she noted that the most recent entry had been made shortly after one o'clock that afternoon, whereas it was now approaching three-thirty.

'I know, I know,' Alice Tremayne muttered as she rushed over to join Adelaide. 'There's nothing important missing, I promise, only we're a bit short-handed this afternoon, because Ellen's transferred to nights.'

'Even so,' Adelaide pointed out, 'Ellen's place should have been taken by one of the night staff, if she's exchanged shifts for her personal convenience.'

'It's not that,' Alice explained. 'Mary Brennan didn't turn up for her shift last night, it seems, and Ellen's covering for her until she shows her face again. The day shift always seems to go more smoothly and Ellen decided that she should throw her hand in with the night shift.'

'But that leaves you one short in here, does it not?' Adelaide queried.

Alice nodded. 'In a sense, yes it does, and it was obviously remiss of us to fall behind a bit in completing the Ward Report, but we're down to five patients now, after Captain Logan was discharged two days ago.'

'He was the one who was blinded?' Adelaide asked and when Alice nodded, she added, 'Was his eyesight fully restored?'

'Yes, thank God, since he was dreading the bandages coming off. But he left here singing your father's praises, and the spirits in here have lifted somewhat since he departed. With the best will in the world he was a difficult patient, and his sour sarcasm always seemed to depress the other patients.'

'Can the three of you manage temporarily if you don't need to fill in the Ward Report after every action?' Adelaide asked.

'Of course, but Miss Nightingale always emphasised the importance of records and in particular statistics relating to medicines administered.'

'I didn't say it wouldn't be completed regularly,' Adelaide said as she slipped her jacket over the back of the chair. 'I may not be a nurse, but I can read and write. May I take it that the entries in the Ward Report are simply taken from information brought back from the beds by the nurses?'

'Yes, but…'

'Yes but nothing,' Adelaide said. 'At last I can feel that I'm really doing something.'

'Which is more than I can,' Matthew muttered at her side.

Adelaide smiled up at him as she replied, 'There's a great deal you can do. First of all, you can escort Miss Drake to her sister's house in Finchley. Then you can go home and check that our daughter's being properly looked after. And if you have any spare time left over, you might wish to visit Captain Logan in the Tower and enquire after his health.'

Padraig Murphy looked up nervously from where he was seated in the room inside Scotland Yard.

'I'm Detective Inspector Jennings,' he was informed. 'And you can guess why you're here, can you not?'

'On the immortal soul of my blessed mother, I haven't a clue,' Murphy replied.

'You're Irish, to judge by your name.'

'Is that an offence?'

'Don't get smart with me or I'll soon make it one. Now — you work in the Tower, do you not?'

'That's right.'

'In the kitchens of the Waterloo Barracks?'

'Again, that's right. What am I supposed to have done?'

'I'm hoping that you'll oblige me by telling me that before you leave this room. Now, the eighteenth of June last, you were working in the kitchens that serve the Officers' Mess inside the Waterloo Barracks, that right?'

'Yes, that's right. The kitchens serve the entire Barracks, but that day we had a private function in the Officers' Mess.'

'The anniversary of the holding of the gates at Waterloo by the Coldstream Guards?'

'It was a special occasion, I know that.'

'And when was the last time that you were in the dining hall prior to the explosion?'

'I wasn't in it at all. I'm a cook and cooks work in the kitchen.'

'I'm well aware of what they're *supposed* to do,' Jennings snapped, 'but I'm suggesting that you found some excuse to go into the dining hall.'

'No, I didn't,' Murphy objected. 'I had enough to do, producing fifteen servings of Beef Wellington. You have to get the pastry to just the right consistency and make sure that you don't take it out of the ovens too early, else it sags —'

'Spare me the cookery lesson,' Jennings interrupted. 'What excuse did you use to go into the dining hall?'

'I didn't, I swear to God! I just told you I didn't, and I can't deny it any more than I already have.'

'When did you first come to London, Murphy?'

'Six years ago now.'

'And where do you live?'

'Tench Street, Wapping. Number fifty-seven. It's a tenement building alongside the London Dock wall.'

'And before that?'

'My cousin's place in Limehouse.'

'Ah — "Bandit Country",' Jennings said knowingly.

'If you say so,' Murphy conceded. 'But it was cheap enough, except my cousin had so many kids and they used to fight with my two, so we were forced to find a place of our own.'

'When was that?'

'Two or more years back. Why the questions about where I live?'

'Had any contact with the Irish community in Bow or Poplar?'

'Those murdering Fenian bastards? Why would I?'

'Because you're Irish, that's why.'

Murphy sighed loudly. 'Here we bloody go again. I was born and raised in a place called Larne — that's in County Antrim, in *Northern* Ireland, a whiles or more north of Belfast. The ones who're demanding that Ireland separate from England are to be found in *Southern* Ireland — a place called Dublin. Not all us Irish want a parting of the ways, which is why I'm here in London.'

'So what brought you to England?' Jennings demanded.

'The ferry — and that's not me being smart. I meant the *actual* ferry, the one that sails backwards and forwards from Larne to Scotland, where I worked as a deckhand until they let me wash the pans in the kitchen on the ferryboat, then learned me how to cook. Then I worked the boats from Belfast to Liverpool, where I hopped ashore one day and found myself a fine billet in the North Western Hotel in Lime Street. That's where I met my wife Rosie, who's from down Limehouse way, and she talked me into coming to London, where I volunteered my skills to the Army. So there you go.'

'And you have no association whatsoever with the Fenians?'

'Do I look stupid?'

'Yes, since you enquire. But you must know people who *are* Fenian supporters.'

44

'Of course I do, but I just feel sorry for them, deluded gombeens that they are.'

'And you were never recruited to assist the Fenian cause, given your very convenient position inside the Tower?'

'They tried, but I managed to persuade them that I'd left my wits in the Jacks, then they left me alone.'

'And who was it who tried to recruit you?'

'The only name I can give you is Eamonn Brennan. He's dangerous, 'cos lots o' eejits believe what he promises them.'

'And where might I find this Eamonn Brennan?'

'A rat hole called "The Harp", in Gun Lane, Limehouse.'

'So you never went into that dining hall on the day of the explosion?'

'On my mother's grave I didn't. But the waiters would have, to set up the tables.'

'Are any of them Irish?'

'Not that I'm aware of. I think a couple are from Russia.'

'Very well, you're free to leave. But we'll be keeping a close eye on you.'

'Thank you kindly. Should you by any unfortunate chance make the acquaintance of Eamonn Brennan, I'd be grateful if you didn't mention that I tipped you the wink.'

An hour later, Jennings reported to Assistant Commissioner Atkinson, as instructed.

'So have you made any progress?' Atkinson demanded.

'Things are moving forward, sir. I've been working closely with Doctor Carlyle at the London Hospital and we've established that the bomb was placed under the table at the celebration dinner. I've also interviewed a man called Murphy who works in the kitchens in the Waterloo Barracks and he gave me a very useful lead to a Fenian stirrer in an Irish hangout in Limehouse called "The Harp". Name of "Brennan". So I've sent a wire to every station in the Met to advise me of anything that comes in with the name of "Brennan" on it. Then I might go in search of a suicide squad to go into The Harp.'

'Leave that to the Irish Branch. You just sit and wait for any intelligence that comes in, understood?'

Jennings didn't have to wait for long. The clock in his office had just clicked round to five p.m. and he was putting papers back into his desk drawers in anticipation of heading home, when a constable loomed in his doorway.

'You wanted anything on "Brennan" — that right, sir?'

'Correct. What have you got me?'

'A dead body, sir. Only it's female. Name of Mary Brennan. They found her facedown in a pile of rubbish up an alleyway off Brick Lane. She's been there some time, they reckon, and she's dressed like she already belonged in a hospital.'

5

By the time that Jennings's police coach had battled its way down through Shoreditch, into Commercial Street, then across into Brick Lane, quite a crowd had gathered, which two uniformed officers were fighting a losing battle to hold back. It was late evening but given the time of year it was still warm, and the sun was only just setting. The police surgeon appeared to have completed his work and was waiting dolefully for Jennings to appear so that he could deliver his provisional findings.

'Single stab wound to the chest, almost certainly penetrated the heart,' he said. 'Death would have been almost instantaneous and no sign of sexual assault. Not a prostitute, to judge by her clothing. She was probably killed a day or so ago. Do you need me any longer?'

'Probably not,' Jennings conceded gloomily as he looked around for further assistance. 'Anyone here from Whitechapel Prison?' he shouted.

A pale-looking middle-aged man raised a hand in acknowledgement. 'Detective Sergeant Pooley — who are you?'

'Detective Inspector Jennings, Scotland Yard. Are you in charge here?'

'Not anymore, if you're here, sir. But why the interest?'

'The woman's name was "Brennan", I'm informed?'

'There are papers in her bag that suggest her name was Mary Brennan, but with an address in some place I've never heard of,' Pooley told him.

The body was at the far end of a narrow alleyway, no more than twenty feet in length, that ran off Brick Lane. It was partly buried under pieces of cloth and empty cardboard rolls, and Jennings raised an eyebrow in Pooley's direction. He already had the answer.

'This alleyway serves the dressmaking business that's through that side door there. The proprietor's already been spoken to and can tell us nothing other than the fact that he uses the alleyway to dump off-cuts and other rubbish. That probably explains why nobody noticed the deceased until the flies began to give her away.'

'They're certainly plentiful, anyway,' Jennings observed sourly as he waved a few from around his face, then studied the body more carefully. The flies appeared to be primarily attracted to the congealed blood on the tunic of the dark blue gown that the corpse was dressed in and were all too visible on the crumpled white panel that ran down its centre, now brown with dried blood. 'Who found the body?' Jennings asked.

'A scavenger — that cove out there in the street being detained by my uniformed constables until he can give a better account of himself. Claims to visit this alleyway regularly in search of things to on-sell in the Saturday markets. Insists that there was no sign of the body yesterday, yet according to the doctor she'd been dead a day or two. His explanation for that is that he only became aware that things weren't quite right when he saw the flies.'

'Sounds reasonable,' Jennings conceded, 'but I'll obviously need a word with him. In the meantime, would I be correct in thinking that the body's dressed like a nurse?'

'That was my conclusion too, sir, and our obliging scavenger also tells us that some nurses live in a rooming house on the next street up — Finch Street — who he often sees walking up and down Brick Lane to and from the direction of the High Street.'

'The London Hospital's down that way,' Jennings said. 'Have there been any reports of missing nurses?'

'None that I'm aware of, sir.'

'Very well. Get the body removed to the mortuary at the London Hospital and lead me to this scavenger.'

'I didn't do nuffin' except find the poor gel, an' that's the 'onest trufe, guvner,' insisted the malodorous man who gave the name of Perkins.

Jennings held his hand up for silence. 'I imagine that you've already told us all that you know, but tell me more about the nurses who live in the next street.'

'Too easy, my friend. They comes up and down Brick Lane all the time, usually in twos and threes. They'm always dressed the same, like that poor lassie down the alleyway back there, an' I think they's comin' to an' from that 'ospital the uvver side o' Whitechapel Road.'

'The London Hospital?'

'No idea what it's called, but yer can't miss it. It's just afore yer gets ter the railway station.'

'Yes, that's the London Hospital right enough. They always walk in twos and threes, you say?'

'Mostly, yeah. But sometimes yer'll see one walkin' by 'erself.'

'Always the same time of day?'

'Twice a day, usually. Sometime after five in the mornin', then seven in the evenin', regular as clockwork. There's usually about an hour between one lot walking down Brick Lane, then another lot walkin' back up it.'

'So cast your mind back two evenings,' Jennings instructed him. 'Did you see any of these nurses walking up or down that evening? Particularly the one whose body you found?'

'Can't say that I did, but I'm not always around 'ere all the time. I works the ground between Aldgate an' Stepney, an' there's lots o' that ter cover.'

'Yes, quite. But you didn't see any nurses that evening, is that what you're telling me?'

'That's right. I were down Commercial Road that evenin'. Nice class o' rubbish down there.'

'Do you happen to know which lodging house the nurses live in?'

'I can point it out ter yer, certainly. It's two up on the left. Yer wanner come wiv me while I shows yer which one?'

'That won't be necessary,' Jennings told him. 'Second on the left from the Brick Lane end of Finch Street, that right?'

Perkins confirmed that this was the case and Jennings gave instructions for the man to be allowed to go after he'd supplied his full name and address, following which the uniformed officers were to take statements from anyone in the immediate vicinity who might be able to supply information. Then he walked a few yards north up Brick Lane and into Finch Street.

Number Four looked like any other common lodging house, with a narrow entrance down one side that led to a rear door behind which was no doubt a communal kitchen. Jennings knew better than to knock and politely await admission to someone who was too obviously a police officer, so he simply walked in and waited by the table in the centre. A drudge of a woman came shuffling out of a room somewhere down the ground-floor hallway and stared him up and down appraisingly before enquiring, 'Yer lookin' fer a bed fer the night?'

'No,' Jennings replied as he displayed his police badge. 'I'm enquiring after a group of nurses who I believe lodge here.'

'What they done?'

'Nothing of which I'm aware. I just need to know if one of them's currently missing.'

'That'll be young Mary. 'Ang about there a minute, an' I'll get Alice fer yer.'

A sleepy young woman appeared in the kitchen, apparently fresh from her bed, to judge by the housecoat wrapped around what Jennings took to be a nightdress.

'You were enquiring about Mary?' she asked as she absentmindedly lit the gas under the pan of water sitting on the cooker. When Jennings confirmed that to be the case, the girl Alice told him: 'We haven't seen her for the past two nights. She and I share a room. Is she in some sort of trouble?'

'The worst kind, I'm afraid. You might want to sit down.' Alice did as requested and Jennings continued, 'We found a young woman's body in an alleyway running off Brick Lane and we think it may be your friend Mary. What did she look like?'

Alice's hands were trembling where they lay folded on the table in front of her as she replied, 'Quite small in stature — maybe five feet two inches tall — with short dark hair. What happened? Did she get run down by a cart or something?'

'There was an address on some papers we found in her bag,' Jennings hedged. 'Does the name "Bangor" mean anything to you?'

'That's where she was from. It's in North Wales, I believe — her hometown.'

'Not Ireland? Only I happen to know that there's a place of the same name in Ireland.'

'No, definitely Wales. We used to poke fun at her for the way she talked, and I knew someone else from Wales who talked in just the same way. So it must be her. She's dead, you said?'

'I'm afraid so. Was she a nurse, by any chance?'

'Yes, like me — we worked alongside each other at the London Hospital. We were both "Nightingale Nurses". How did she come to die?'

'I'm afraid I'm not at liberty to tell you, Miss…?'

'Tremayne. Alice Tremayne. Are you *sure* it's her?'

'Almost certain, from what you tell me, although she's not been formally identified.'

'Her family's still back in Wales, but there's a brother somewhere nearby — somewhere in Bow, I believe. I can get you the address if you give me a moment or two.'

'That won't be necessary, Miss Tremayne,' Jennings replied gently. 'If you tell me she was a nurse at the London Hospital, then I can think of someone else who can carry out the identification. Thank you for your assistance, and I'm sorry to be the bearer of such bad tidings.'

'It's probably Violet Dunning, back to retrieve that umbrella she left here earlier,' Adelaide suggested as she rose with a sigh from her chair in the living room and headed for the front door to answer the knocking.

'I'm really sorry to be troubling you at this late hour,' Jennings apologised as he stood at the open doorway, twisting his pork pie hat in his hands, 'but we've found the body of a young woman in an alleyway in Whitechapel, and we have reason to believe that she may be one of your nurses.'

'They're not *my* nurses, Inspector, they're Miss Nightingale's, but are you by any chance referring to Mary Brennan?'

'You knew?'

'Only that she'd been missing for a few days. Do you think it may be her?'

'We have good reason to believe she may be, yes.'

'And you wish me to identify her?'

'If you'd be so good. She's in your father's mortuary.'

'I'll need my hat and coat — just wait there a moment,' Adelaide instructed him as she walked back down the hallway and into the living room, where Matthew sat with raised eyebrows.

'That sounded like Jennings.'

'It is, and I have to go out. I hope not to be long. If Florence wakes up while I'm gone, there are some pieces of apple ready cut and lying on a plate in the pantry — second shelf.'

In the police coach heading west down Mile End Road, Adelaide voiced her concern. 'Given that this is a police matter, may I assume that she didn't die of natural causes?'

'She didn't, I'm afraid. It looks as if she was stabbed to death. Did you know her well?'

'Hardly at all. She was one of the nurses on the night shift in the Tower Ward looking after those wounded Guardsmen, and I barely even spoke to her. From memory, a rather sweet little girl with an engaging smile and big brown eyes — short dark hair and spoke with a funny sort of accent.'

'Irish?'

'I wouldn't know — could that be important?'

'Very, given that her name's common in Ireland and we're currently investigating the activities of a man with the same name who may be behind the bombing itself.'

Given the lack of other vehicles at that time in the late evening, they reached the hospital within minutes and Jennings led the way down into the basement where the mortuary was located.

Carlyle raised weary eyes towards the door as they entered, then frowned. 'Was this really necessary, Inspector?' he demanded as he hastily threw a large white sheet over the form on the dissection table.

'Absolutely,' Jennings insisted. 'I want there to be no doubt who she is before I continue my investigations. Adelaide, if you'd be so good?'

Adelaide walked steadily towards the table and gritted her teeth firmly together as her father lowered the sheet far enough to reveal the face. Adelaide blanched, then nodded. 'That's Mary Brennan, as I remember her, but with very little colour remaining in her face. Exsanguination?'

'Extreme,' her father confirmed. 'Single thrust to the upper torso with a heavy and sharp blade, possibly a sword. It shattered through three ribs and punctured the pericardium. The only blessing is that it would have been instant.'

'So she was stabbed to death?' Jennings asked.

Carlyle nodded. 'Now you have both her identity and her cause of death, you can probably call it a night. I intend to, and I'll take Adelaide home in my coach.'

Jennings took his leave, still carrying his hat, and Carlyle lit the gas under the water flask. 'Let's have some hot chocolate, shall we? Then tell me how you're doing in your new role.'

'Quite well, so far as I can tell,' Adelaide told him a few moments later as he repeated the question after handing her the spoon to stir the sugar into her mug. 'The girls don't seem to resent my presence, which is probably because the alternative would be Miss Nightingale herself.'

'You underestimate yourself, which, if I may say with all the love of a doting father, is unusual for you. As is your newfound tact and gentle firmness. Two or three years ago, I would have said that you were the last person on earth to be placed in a position over other young ladies that required a diplomatic approach.'

Adelaide chuckled. 'Was I *so* bad?'

'I'm afraid so, and it's a mark of Matthew's courage and powers of perseverance that he hung in there, dodged the verbal bullets and waited until you were ready for marriage.'

'Dear, darling Matthew,' Adelaide said over the rim of her mug. 'He's still the most infuriating, and at times hopelessly impractical, idiot, but he's opened up a side of my life I'd never even contemplated. I feel sorry for my nurses, who seem destined never to find the happiness that I have. Which reminds me — I need to tell them about Mary, before they read all about it in tomorrow's newspapers.'

She finished her mug of hot chocolate and promised to return for the coach home after a brief journey up to the Tower Ward. She took the two flights of stairs and walked softly through the heavy rubber swing doors into the ward, then froze at the sight that confronted her.

Inspector Jennings was seated at the centre desk, with the remaining night shift nurses grouped around him, all with pale faces. Ellen Tring was looking grim and resentful, while Edith Crawford was sobbing quietly into a handkerchief. Near the entrance to the ward, in Bed Six, Lieutenant Hargraves was calling feebly, but unsuccessfully, for a nurse.

Adelaide strode determinedly down the ward and raised her voice angrily. 'I really must register my disapproval, Inspector Jennings! These young ladies are dedicated to relieving the sufferings of others, but that doesn't mean that they are impervious to suffering of their own. You blunder in here late at night like a runaway carthorse and have no doubt caused them considerable distress with the lack of tact for which you are renowned throughout the Metropolitan Police service. What can these poor girls tell you that I haven't already?'

'I'll have no idea unless I ask them, will I?' Jennings retorted angrily. 'They almost certainly knew the dead girl better than you did, and I strongly suspect that she had sinister Irish connections. If you want to find out how and why she died, then I'm your best bet!'

'The "dead girl", as you call her, had a name and a dedication to saving lives. Her name was Mary Brennan and she was *nursing* soldiers, not killing them!'

'What you may not be aware of,' Jennings hissed back as he lowered his voice, 'is that one of the names I've been given as a possible lead to those who caused that Tower explosion is also called "Brennan". I'm informed that he holds court in a disreputable pub in Limehouse. And the late Mary Brennan had a brother living in the Bow area, or so I'm informed by the girl who shared a room with her. You can hardly expect me to ignore that connection, can you?'

'Alice was obviously the one who told you about Mary's brother in Bow,' Ellen Tring announced coldly. 'That hardly qualifies her as a reliable police informer, since we all knew about him and to the best of my knowledge Mary had very little to do with him. And I'm not even sure if it was Bow anyway — it could have been anywhere in that general area of the East End.'

'Like Limehouse, you mean?' Jennings countered. 'It seems to me that there's much regarding the recent activities of Mary Brennan that demands further investigation.'

'But not in here!' Adelaide insisted sharply. 'This is a hospital ward dedicated to the nursing of badly injured Guardsmen, Inspector, all of whom were serving Queen and country. I'll undertake to obtain as much information as I can regarding

Mary Brennan from Miss Nightingale, who trained her and sent her here. In the meantime, you'd be better off conducting street enquiries regarding how it was possible for a young lady who was obviously tending to the sick to be knifed to death in the streets that you and the rest of Scotland Yard are supposed to be keeping safe. So off you go — now!'

Their eyes met in a contest of wills, during which Jennings concluded that he was unlikely to get any other meaningful information from the four thoroughly rattled nurses on the night shift, so he had nothing to lose by making a dignified retreat.

'I've by no means finished here,' he warned them as he rose from the table and gave Adelaide one more defiant look before striding out of the ward.

6

The desk sergeant looked up languidly from his morning newspaper, then became more alert when he read the name and rank displayed on the police badge that was flapped open under his nose.

'Who's the most senior detective on duty?' Jennings demanded curtly, far from impressed at being distracted from his attempts to show the Irish Branch how it was done by the need to divert his attention to the murder of a nurse. When advised that it was Sergeant Pooley and that he could be found one floor up, Jennings declined the offer of a uniformed escort and loped up the stairs alone.

'Is the tea around here any good?' he asked in the doorway to the office that Pooley appeared to share with two others. Pooley shook his head but invited Jennings to accompany him back outside, to the cafe on the corner of Leman Street, only a few doors down from the station.

'Did anything come of the additional enquiries?' Jennings demanded as he sipped his tea and probed his bacon sandwich with a knife for signs of meat.

Pooley grimaced. 'This is the East End, remember? Folk have more things to keep quiet about down here than they have reasons to tell the truth. But you might try "Hadleys the Butchers" at the junction of Brick Lane and Montague Street, if only to deter old Jack Hadley from haunting our front desk.'

'And why might that be?'

'He claims to be the target of some weird cove who's ambition is to drive him potty, parading up and down outside his shop, glaring through his display window, but never coming in to buy.'

'You think he may have something useful to tell us?'

'It'll be a first if he has. But there's always the chance that he might be describing someone staking out those nurses as they passed to and fro down Brick Lane on their way to the hospital on Whitechapel Road.'

'That smelly old scavenger struck me as someone with an unhealthy interest in watching nurses coming and going,' Jennings muttered. 'Did he turn out to be kosher?'

'The beat men reckon that they see him every day going about his grubby business, anyway, and it's not an offence to look. Added to which, the girls would smell him long before he could leap out of his hiding place at them.'

'You're probably right about that,' Jennings replied, 'but you have to admit that it was a pretty audacious business and that whoever did it must have been very patient, biding his time until the one he was after came along on her own, all the time keeping close and hidden at the end of that alleyway.'

'You reckon he knew the girl he attacked — it wasn't just a random job?'

'I'd put money on it,' Jennings asserted. 'She had an Irish name and seems to have had a brother in that part of the East End where all those Fenian bastards hang out. My money's on her knowing something of what led to that bombing in the Tower, which was why she was done in — to silence her.'

'So you're still in charge of the case?'

'For the time being anyway, unless and until we find that the death of the nurse and the Tower bombing aren't connected.'

'So you'll go and talk to Jack Hadley?'

'I'm on my way once I can chew this sandwich into submission — might even pick up some chops for supper while I'm at it.'

Jennings' provisional plan to have chops for supper evaporated the moment that he caught sight of the display under the glass, the items in question being an unhealthy brown that was indicative of long exposure to the air. The same was true of most of the other items that lay on either side of the chops, and the state of the sawdust on the floor betrayed the fact that the proprietor was not an enthusiast with a broom.

'What can I get for you?' Jack Hadley asked hopefully as the previous customer departed, clutching a paper package of lambs' liver.

'Answers to questions,' Jennings told him as he raised his police badge to eye level.

'I haven't done anything wrong, so far as I'm aware,' Hadley protested.

Jennings raised both eyebrows. 'You couldn't say that to a health inspector, I'll warrant, but I'm here in connection with your complaint about a man lurking outside your shop. You'd have to hope he's not with the Council.'

'It's about bloody time *somebody* paid attention to my complaints,' Hadley fired back. 'I pay a lot in rates to stay in business here, and blokes like him hanging around are inclined to put people off looking in my window.'

'I was put off by what I could see in there,' Jennings replied with a curl of his lower lip, 'but tell me more about your unwanted admirer.'

'He started by loitering around across the street, looking towards the shop. Then he developed the habit of walking across from time to time and staring into the display window, like he was looking to buy something. Always the same time of day, roughly — while I was getting ready to close for the day.'

'And when exactly *do* you close for the day, Mr Hadley?'

'When I can tell that I'm not likely to get any more customers. People often drop in for something for their tea on their way home from work. That's when the man always seems to be hanging around, putting people off.'

'So, early evening?'

'Yes, about then.'

'In the early morning as well, while people are on their way *to* work?'

'No, never then.'

'And these people you see coming home from work, do they include nurses from the London Hospital?'

'I wouldn't know where they're from, but I sometimes see young women walking past my window wearing what look like nurses' uniforms.'

'So this man's always around when folk are coming up Brick Lane on their way home from work, that it?'

'Yeah. So what are you going to do about him?'

'Lock him up, if he's who I think he is. But I've got a few more questions before we get to that happy moment.'

'Ask away.'

'You heard about the dreadful murder just up the street there?'

'The lassie who got herself stabbed to death up that alleyway? Dreadful business. *She* was a nurse as well, they reckon.'

'Ever see her walking past your shop?'

'Might have done. They all look the same to me.'

'And this man who you're complaining about, who lurks outside your shop as people are coming home from work every day — what does he look like?'

'Couldn't tell you exactly, since he always keeps his face hidden, like he's ashamed of it or something. Big black hat pulled low over his face and a long black cloak down nearly to his boots. He reminds me of one of those cut-throats who you read about that used to stalk the Ratcliffe Highway, down the road there in Wapping. Is it true that the dead lassie had *her* throat cut?'

'Who told you that?'

'It's the talk of the street, and there's even talk that the Ripper's come back.'

'Talk can be dangerous at times, and this is one of them,' Jennings muttered. 'How tall is this man you're describing?'

'Quite tall, I'd reckon. Taller than me by a good couple of inches, so maybe approaching six feet.'

'You ever hear him talk?'

'Never.'

'And how long has he been hanging about in the street out there?'

'Two weeks or so, maybe a bit less.'

'You recall hearing all about that explosion in the Tower Barracks?'

'Of course — it was all anyone talked about for a day or two afterwards.'

'Was it before or after that when the man made his first appearance, so far as you're aware?'

'After. Definitely after, because the lad who used to work for me was all set to join the Army, then changed his mind after the explosion. He still left all the same, and I got my daughter to come in and help me until I could replace him. The bloke in the hat and cloak gave my daughter a right old scare when he first stared through the window at her. She reckoned he had a funny look in his eyes.'

'So she got a good look at his face?'

'Yeah, but she's not here anymore. She went back to her husband's pig farm in Essex, and as you can see I've got a new lad helping me out.'

'Very well. You're sure there's nothing more you can tell me?'

'Not really. So what are you going to do about him?'

'I might come back this evening and see if he returns, but even if he does I can't arrest him for walking up and down the street. However, if I'm right in the opinion I'm forming as the result of your invaluable assistance, I don't think he'll be back.'

'You reckon he's lost interest in my shop?'

'He never *was* interested in your shop, Mr Hadley — only the people who were coming and going past it. Good day to you.'

Back out on the pavement Jennings was debating whether or not to return to Leman Street and instruct that an extra uniformed constable be positioned at the foot of Brick Lane when he was accosted by a smart-looking man wearing a loud checked suit and a Brown Derby hat.

'It's Inspector Jennings, isn't it? Come to flush out the Ripper?'

Jennings gritted his teeth and glared at the man, who, far from discouraged, extracted a business card from his waistcoat pocket and handed it over.

'Aubrey Buchanan, from the *Illustrated London News*. We met when you were exposing all that nonsense about the spirits of the dead allegedly returning from a plague pit. Now it seems that you're hunting down another ghost from the past.'

'Meaning?'

'Meaning our old friend Jack the Ripper,' Buchanan said.

Jennings grabbed the man by the lapels of his gaudy jacket. 'Are you the one who's been spreading that rubbish around the streets? If so, I'll lock you up for interfering with a police investigation!'

Buchanan smiled grimly as he prised Jennings's hands from his lapels and shook his head. 'I got that information from the police at the scene of that ghastly murder up the side of Prestons' dressmaking business.'

'I was there myself, in charge of the investigation and none of us said anything about the Ripper.'

'That's not what I heard,' Buchanan smirked. 'You can seek to deny it now if you wish, but my informant was quite adamant that he heard one of the police officers standing by the body say that it looked like the work of the Ripper. And the Met never caught him, did they? And this latest victim — a nurse still dressed in her uniform, as I understand it — she was viciously stabbed, was she not, just like all the Ripper's victims?'

'Any comparison between how she died and the way that the Ripper disposed of his victims is purely superficial,' Jennings insisted.

Buchanan smirked back at him. 'So a knife *was* involved? That would be consistent with the considerable amount of blood that my informant saw on her body when he first found it.'

'If you want to base your over-dramatised published fantasies on the word of a smelly old vagrant, then be my guest. But you won't get a word of confirmation from me.'

'And how long before he strikes again?' Buchanan challenged him. 'The public have the right to know that he's back at large.'

'I obviously have no way of knowing if there'll be any more attacks,' Jennings reasoned, 'but I *can* tell you that I'll have your arse in a cell if you write anything designed to alarm the public without justification.'

'And on that note, I'll take my leave of you,' Buchanan said as he raised his hat mockingly in a provocative gesture, then left Jennings standing alone on the pavement in the middle of the morning, blaspheming loudly until taken to task by a passing clergyman.

'I understand that you were already advised that Mary Brennan was missing from her post,' Adelaide said quietly as she looked across the desk at Florence Nightingale, 'but we obviously had no idea at that stage that she'd met such a tragic end. I'm sorry. I should have kept a closer eye on what your nurses were doing once they finished their duties for the day.'

'My dear, you're their supervisor, not their mother,' Florence reminded her. 'For all you know she was off to meet her young man, and you wouldn't presume to poke your nose into her personal relationships, now would you?'

'As far as I can tell, she was walking home from her night shift,' Adelaide told her. 'She would have left the hospital sometime shortly after six o'clock on the morning that she was murdered, and given the distance between the hospital and where her body was found, her attacker must have struck sometime a little before seven in the morning. The street must have been full of people on their way to work, and it would have been broad daylight. But nobody reported seeing a thing and her body wasn't found for a day and a half after that, because it was partly obscured by rubbish in the alleyway into which her body had been thrown.'

'And how could you have prevented any of that?' Florence asked gently.

Adelaide shook her head. 'I'm not sure, but perhaps if I'd insisted that the girls only walk out and about in twos or threes?'

'A further constraint on their already restricted lives? Would they have been likely to obey you?'

'That's what they're doing now, at my suggestion,' Adelaide replied. 'Did I overstep my authority, do you think?'

'Far from it — you merely demonstrated a worthy and appropriate concern for their welfare,' she was reassured. 'But you weren't to know that someone would make a random target of Mary, were you?'

'But was it random?' Adelaide asked. 'A certain Inspector Jennings from Scotland Yard is investigating that dreadful bomb explosion that led to the opening of the Tower Ward and the need for your nurses, and he seems to think that there might be a connection.'

'*Our* nurses, dear,' Florence corrected her.

Adelaide nodded. 'You're very kind, but the fact remains that Mary Brennan had the misfortune to have a common Irish surname, and this Inspector Jennings informs me that he's been given the same name — this time that of a man believed to be in charge of the Fenians who're suspected of being behind the bombing. I tried to assure him that poor Mary was from somewhere in Wales, but he seems determined to drag even her memory into the ... well, the responsibility for what happened in the Tower. I sort of promised him that I'd find out all I could about her background.'

'It just so happens that I recently sent a letter of condolence to her parents, advising them of what a credit she was to them and how she lived her life selflessly in the service of others.

Her personal file is still on the desk here, so let me assist.' Florence looked long and hard at the contents of the brown folder that she lifted from the far edge of her desk, then looked back up at Adelaide. 'She was certainly of Irish parentage, but no more than that, so far as I can see from the personal details she gave me when I first interviewed her for a place in my nursing school. Her father was a farmer in a place called "Drogheda" who came over here in search of a living when the last famine wiped out his livelihood. He was employed as the manager of a sheep run in North Wales — near a town called "Bangor" — and so far as I can see from what's written here, Mary never even visited Ireland in her lifetime. So she seems to have been Welsh rather than Irish.'

'That's how I remember her,' Adelaide recalled softly as she stemmed a tear that threatened. 'So I can tell Inspector Jennings that her death was at the hands of some random lunatic walking the streets in search of a victim?'

'You can tell *him*, certainly, but I urge you not to put it in those terms to her former colleagues, for fear of alarming them that another "Jack the Ripper" might be on the loose.'

'And may I also tell them that you'll be sending them a replacement for Mary?'

'Indeed you may. Her name's Phyllis Collier and she's already had some ward experience here at St Thomas's. She should be arriving tomorrow or the day after.'

'Excellent news!' Adelaide said warmly. 'She can go onto the night shift and allow Ellen Tring back onto days. Then I needn't spend half my days ensuring that the Ward Report's being kept up to date.'

'You've been sharing duties with your nurses?'

'Not nursing duties, obviously. But Ellen's transfer to nights left her team one short, and I realised that by undertaking the record-keeping by which you set such great store I could free up the nurses for what they're best trained to do.'

'Excellent, my dear. I am reassured that when I appointed you I was not mistaken in my judgment. Give the girls my warmest regards when you return to them.'

'I will, of course. But the best news I can give them is that their numbers will be back to the appropriate level for the work they're called upon to do.'

'We haven't yet even discussed the current condition of the patients,' Florence reminded her.

'I'm not qualified to speak of their medical condition, obviously.'

'Obviously not, but you overlook what in many ways is the more important matter of how they're bearing up mentally and spiritually. A healthy mind and spirit is just as important to a speedy recovery as medicine.'

'As far as that goes, they all appear to be in fine spirits,' Adelaide reassured her. 'The first of them was released last week, having regained his eyesight despite terrible facial scarring. His discharge seemed to lift the spirits of the others, particularly since he was not the most popular among them and had a somewhat doleful turn of mind. As for the rest, I was able to be the means by which a man with severe chest wounds was reunited with his fiancée, and most of the remainder of the men have at least received visits from their wives, thanks to my husband's regular visits to the Tower Barracks, to encourage them to do so. We hope to discharge one or two of them by the end of this month, then we may have to consider new placements for the nurses.'

'I have no doubt that the London Hospital will wish to retain their services,' Florence predicted, 'but I shall rely on you to ensure that they remain in their teams. Morale is so important in our profession, I think you'll agree, so don't let me delay you in returning to your colleagues. And thank you again, so much, for fulfilling my faith in you.'

'It's more a matter of *me* thanking *you* for allowing me to find my proper role in life,' Adelaide said as she rose to leave.

Back at the hospital, Adelaide entered the Tower Ward to find Matthew seated at the desk in the middle of the ward, surrounded by the nurses from the day shift who were clearly entranced by the presence of the handsome young clergyman. Adelaide coughed loudly, and the girls dispersed hurriedly among the beds down either side of the ward as she strode down to the desk with raised eyebrows. 'Well?' she demanded, hands on hips.

Matthew grinned. 'Two things. First of all, I'd like to take the most beautiful woman I know out for a cup of tea and a sandwich. But you can come along as well, if you wish.'

Adelaide chuckled despite herself, but kept up the stern facial expression. 'And what was your second reason for coming in here to distract my nurses from their duties?'

'I'm visiting the Tower Barracks today, and I was enquiring if any of your patients might have messages I could relay to their wives.'

'Hmm,' Adelaide responded. 'Well, go ahead and do that, if you haven't already, and then I have a message for you from *your* wife.'

'Yes?'

'Yes. She's too busy in here to accept your invitation to go out to a cafe. But you can bring me something that tastes like tea, along with a sandwich that has recently become associated with cheese. Off you go, and don't dawdle in order to sweet talk any more nurses.'

7

Jennings barely had time to look up to identify the shadow that had just darkened his open office doorway before a newspaper came skidding across the table towards him, having been thrown by his visitor.

'What did you think you were about?' Assistant Commissioner Atkinson snapped as he glared down at him.

Jennings looked down with a groan as he recognised the banner at the top of the front page of that week's *Illustrated London News* and read the massive headline just below it.

HAS THE RIPPER RETURNED?

The gruesome discovery of a young woman's severely lacerated corpse up a secluded alleyway off Whitechapel's Brick Lane has instilled in the local population a fear that the beast known as "Jack the Ripper" has returned to his old haunts.

As readers will recall with a shiver of horror, it has been less than ten years since this murderous lunatic prowled the streets of London's East End in search of young women to mutilate. Although his sickening activities appeared to cease for a while, the Metropolitan Police never once confirmed that they had buckled the maniac and it appears that he is still free to wreak his terrible actions on unsuspecting women walking our more shadowy streets late at night.

In search of the truth, our intrepid correspondent Aubrey Buchanan took himself to the site of this latest outrage and there spoke with Inspector John Jennings of Scotland Yard. After conceding that 'The Ripper' had never been brought to trial, Inspector Jennings was also obliged to admit that this latest victim — believed to be a nurse from the nearby London

Hospital — had been savagely attacked with a knife and that officers at the scene had remarked that it looked like the work of the man who held the East End in a state of mortal terror for many months within the memory of most of those reading this. Inspector Jennings was also obliged to admit that there could be more such attacks in the immediate future.

The citizens of our proud capital are entitled to better service from our police than this. Instead of employing their billy clubs to beat the heads of innocent men and women whose only offence is to live in the depths of poverty and in dire need of safe accommodation, they should be ensuring that this homicidal lunatic is safely buckled before he can strike again. So come on, Commissioner Bradford — earn your scandalously large remuneration and prove that we have a police force worthy of that name and capable of capturing and silencing just one man.

'What on earth possessed you to agree to meet with this drivelling idiot?' Atkinson demanded, his face crimson with rage.

'I *didn't*.' Jennings explained. 'I was down there making enquiries when he accosted me in the street.'

'And *did* you tell him that it looked like the work of the Ripper?'

'Of course not. The poor girl was stabbed to death, that's all.'

'And you presumably *did* concede that we couldn't rule out any further attacks?'

'I could hardly tell him otherwise, could I? Not while retaining any credibility as a police officer.'

'And what are you doing to find the man responsible? I assume that it *was* a man?'

'I'd imagine so, to judge by the ferocity of the wound.'

'I don't want your "imaginings", Inspector — I want this man caught without delay! Is that clearly understood?'

'Yes, sir. As it happens, I believe that the death of this girl — Mary Brennan, her name was — may be linked with the Tower bombings that I'm already investigating.'

'Not anymore you're not. Concentrate on finding this killer — today, for preference — and leave the Tower business to the Irish Branch. Clear?'

'Yes, sir.'

'Well, get on with it! And if there's one more piece like this anywhere in the pages of this scandal sheet, you'll be out of a job!'

He stormed out before Jennings could think of any appropriate response. Instead, he hurled a pencil through the open doorway recently vacated by the Assistant Commissioner and let fly a stream of invective.

He reluctantly re-read Buchanan's piece in the newspaper that Atkinson had left behind. Below it was a reprinted artist's impression entitled 'The Ripper Stalks His Next Victim', from an 1888 issue of the same scandal sheet, and Jennings cursed even more loudly when he realised that Buchanan had skilfully sailed so close to the wind that it was impossible to point to a single positive untruth in what he had written.

Jennings was also uncomfortably aware that it had been he who had made reference to the Ripper, while chiding Pooley for his naivety in searching for a motive for the slaughter. He must have been overheard and misinterpreted by that wretch of a scavenger, who had in turn conveyed the same garbled message to Buchanan. It was all nonsense, but he could not prove that Buchanan had not been given the Ripper suggestion in good faith.

Likewise, Jennings *had* been obliged to concede that no-one could ever guarantee that there would be no further attacks in an area of London notorious for mindless violence. And it was true that they never *had* brought the Ripper to trial, although the rumours that floated around the Yard as to the reason for that were as fanciful as they were numerous.

No, there was nothing that Jennings could charge Buchanan with, the slimy bastard. One could only hope that whoever had done for Mary Brennan suddenly took a strong aversion to gutter journalists. At least he was relieved of the Tower bombing investigation, which freed up his time to prove that this latest knifing could not possibly have been the work of Jack the Ripper. He could start by picking the brains of the finest surgeon he knew. With a sigh he reached for his hat and headed out for the London Hospital.

Matthew walked carefully down the row of identical-looking front doors in the courtyard of dwellings allocated to the families of Tower Guard officers, searching for Number 11. Having found it in the centre of the row, he pulled firmly on the brass doorknocker and hit it twice. There was the sound of bustling movement just behind it, and a harassed-looking woman opened it from the inside with soapy hands and an anguished expression. She met Matthew's gaze for a moment, then her face lost all its colour as she took in his dog collar and anticipated the worst. 'Is it Tom? Have you come from the hospital?'

'Have no fear, Mrs Curran,' Matthew said. 'It's not bad news, but I *have* just come from the hospital, with good news from your husband. You *are* Mrs Curran, I take it?'

'That's me. Good news, you said? Come inside, but pardon the mess. It's washing day.'

Matthew eased past the boiling tub just inside the door alongside the mangle and followed Rose Curran into her parlour, where two young children who might have passed for twins were arguing volubly over ownership rights to a bowling hoop. Mrs Curran ordered them both outside, waved Matthew into a padded armchair that had some of its stuffing open to view, and enquired eagerly after the good news.

Matthew told her, 'Your husband's making great progress and hopes to be discharged from the hospital within a week or so.'

'God be praised!' Rose Curran said. 'The children have been missing him. And so have I, of course, although things will be different once he's home. We'll have to move out of here, since Tom'll no longer be a soldier, which is a good thing in some ways, but...' She paused.

'That's the other good news,' Matthew said. 'Your husband was visited in hospital by his brother from Reading, who as you know has a provisions store there. He's offered Tom a position as the manager of a new market garden he's recently opened up and is doing very well selling vegetables direct to the locals.'

'Oh, that's *wonderful* news!' Rose Curran's shoulders began to heave and she gave way to sobs of relief. She tried to stem the flowing tears with a hand still wet with soap suds, then gave Matthew a weak smile of thanks as he extracted a clean pocket handkerchief and handed it across to her. She regained control and grinned self-consciously. 'I'm sorry, Reverend, but you've no idea what a worry it's been, wondering what we'd do for money now that poor old Tom only has one arm and can't be a soldier anymore. I couldn't have wished for better news, and here I am not even offering you a cup of tea. I can send one of the kids out for cake as well, if you'd like some.'

'No need, thank you, Mrs Curran. I'm only too glad to have been able to bring you such happy tidings. Sometimes, in my line of work, I'm conveying the worst sort of news, so please don't go to any trouble on my account.'

'God bless you, young man!' Rose gushed as she reached out and took his hand in hers. 'Pardon the soap suds, but at least my hand's clean. Can I give you a donation to your church or something, or are you Army?'

'I'm the curate of St Dunstan's, up the road in Stepney, but please keep your money. If you want to thank anyone, thank God, and perhaps we'll see you at one of our services. Now, if you'll excuse me, I have to be on my way.'

'Yes, of course, and thank you yet again, you lovely man!' Rose gushed as she waved her hand towards the door. She followed close behind him as he was leaving, and just after he'd bid her a final farewell she suddenly leaned forward and kissed him on the cheek. 'That's for you, not your church,' she said.

Matthew reddened slightly, then stepped back out into the courtyard. He'd only gone a few steps further down and was approaching the door to Number 3 when it opened and a man slipped furtively out into the courtyard ahead of him. A woman was smilingly waving him goodbye while fastening up her blouse, and her face flushed bright red with guilt when she saw Matthew approaching. He was searching his memory for why her face seemed familiar when she broke the silence.

'Well, what d'you expect? I need to put money on the table and what with that useless lump of a husband being in the hospital, I had to do *something* to make ends meet, what with all the debts he's left me.'

'It's Mrs Logan, isn't it?' Matthew asked, unsure what else to say.

She nodded. 'I suppose I should ask how Gerard's doing. Have you by any chance been visiting him in hospital?'

Matthew did his best to keep the confusion and concern from his face. 'Were you not told that he was discharged last week? His eyesight's been restored, I'm delighted to say.'

'Thanks for the warning,' Mary Logan said. 'A bloody good job he didn't show up here half an hour ago, else the feathers would have flown.'

'You mean he hasn't been home yet?' Matthew asked. 'Do you think that something bad might have happened to him?'

'Him?' Mary replied cynically. 'The only bad thing that ever happens to him is when he can't play cards anymore because he's out of money. The chances are that he's holed up — in more senses than one — in that whorehouse along the Thames where he loses most of his money. What's it called again? "The Shamrock", that's it, I think. Down in Shadwell somewhere. Anyway, if you find him, tell him not to bother coming home.'

Shocked and not a little embarrassed, Matthew quickened his pace as he made his way out of the Waterloo Barracks area of the Tower complex and mingled with the sightseers. Then he chided himself that he was only delaying the moment when he was obliged to return to a house that was empty of Adelaide during every day and with a reluctant sigh of acceptance he turned his steps towards the Bell Tower and the main exit.

'It's a little early for tea,' Carlyle told Jennings as his head appeared around the mortuary door. 'Added to which the place is somewhat malodorous even by your standards, thanks to the drowning case that your Whitechapel colleagues sent over this morning. The man drowned all right — in his own vomit, probably, prior to falling into the Thames. But come in anyway.'

Jennings extracted his pocket handkerchief and held it over his nose, then attempted to be heard through the filter. He tried several times, then finally removed the cover with a frustrated noise and invited Carlyle outside. 'Outside the hospital, I mean,' he added. 'The cafeteria upstairs is about as healthy as the air in here, and I'm prepared to pay for your advice with a cup of real tea and perhaps even a meat pie, if you haven't yet dined.'

'So what aspect of my advice is as valuable as a mutton pie?' Carlyle asked above the rattle and rumble of the traffic passing along Whitechapel Road as they sat outside at the pavement cafe across from the hospital.

'That lass who was knifed to death a few days ago — the one who Adelaide identified as one of her nurses,' Jennings replied. 'Please tell me that she wasn't another victim of Jack the Ripper.'

Carlyle smiled. 'Isn't it *your* job to find out who killed her?'

'Obviously, but some local busybody's written a piece in that dreadful *London News* rag trying to claim that the Ripper's back in town.'

'But you know better, do you not?'

'Only the rumours that run up and down the corridors inside the Yard. What I need from you is something I can use to prove that Mary Brennan's death wasn't the work of the same lunatic.'

Carlyle thought for a moment, swirling his tea absent-mindedly around the bottom of his mug, while Jennings's attention was drawn to the sight of a uniformed constable hurrying through the front doors to the London Hospital. Finally, Carlyle had organised his thoughts. 'Well, the most obvious thing, to my mind anyway, is that Mary Brennan died from one heavy sword thrust through the heart, from the front, whereas the Ripper victims, from what I've read, had their throats slit from behind. Then, of course, there were the attempts by the Ripper to remove organs from his victims' bodies. Again I can only rely on the post-mortem reports that are on file and which I studied in order to demonstrate to my students what bad surgery looks like. From what I could read, the suggestion that the Ripper possessed surgical experience was an overheated exaggeration. He knew where the body parts he was after were located, that's all, and had any student of mine performed extractions like that I'd have recommended that he leave my class and transfer his skills to an abattoir. Are you listening, since you paid good money for this advice?'

'Yes, sorry,' Jennings replied as he took his gaze away from the sight of the same uniformed police officer running from the hospital and blowing his whistle to attract attention. Other uniforms came into sight and they formed a huddle in the roadway before one of them set off running westwards along Whitechapel Road in the general direction of Leman Street.

'There's then the matter of the choice of victim,' Carlyle continued as he regained Jennings's attention. 'She was female, of course, but there the comparison ends. Mary Brennan was obviously a nurse, to judge by her clothing, and it would seem that she was killed in the early morning, whereas the Ripper victims were all selected during the hours of darkness.'

'But a solitary female, walking alone?' Jennings challenged him.

Carlyle nodded. 'As I said, the only similarity. The Ripper selected victims who were alone in the early hours of the morning in a low part of the city. This, by definition, almost guaranteed that they were prostitutes, which is why the press at the time — and, I believe, certain elements of the Met — concluded that he had a "down" on women of that calling. Mary Brennan, on the other hand, was a respectable girl walking home from work in broad daylight.'

'Do you think her killer knew her?' Jennings asked.

Carlyle shrugged. 'Perhaps, but she was singled out for a reason. I don't believe that she just happened to come along at random when the man lying in wait was feeling homicidal. She was staked out and killed for a reason, Inspector. *Now* what?'

They both looked across the road, where loud voices could suddenly be heard. A police wagon rolled to a halt in the forecourt of the hospital and several uniformed constables raced towards its front doors. Jennings was already half on his feet when he spotted a handcart being hurried into the same forecourt by a breathless civilian, led by another uniformed officer who was clearing a path for him.

'Finish your pie quickly,' Jennings instructed Carlyle, 'because I believe we have urgent business across the road. *Both* of us.'

Adelaide was busy introducing the new recruit. 'This is Phyllis Collier,' she told the nurses grouped around the centre table, 'and she'll be taking poor Mary's place on the night shift. This will allow Ellen to return to days and then I can go back to being a mother again, as well as visiting other hospitals where Nightingale Nurses are serving. Hopefully she'll be able to share the room in the boarding house with Alice here, like Mary did.'

'I'd be delighted,' Alice said. 'To be perfectly honest, it's been a bit lonely — and a little bit spooky — in there all on my own for the past few days. I don't get home until after you've left, of course, but even having your clothing and other possessions around me will be a bit more reassuring.'

'As for the duties,' Adelaide continued as she smiled reassuringly at Phyllis, 'Ellen, or Edith, or one of the other night nurses can explain those to you. As you can see, all the patients are male and they're recovering at different speeds from the injuries they sustained during that dreadful explosion at the Tower Barracks. Anyway, Phyllis, you should probably get yourself up to your new accommodation and secure a few hours of shut-eye before you commence duties at six o'clock this evening.'

'Here's Mary's spare room key,' Alice said as she handed it over. 'The bed by the window is yours, and I did my best to leave things tidy when I set out this morning.'

Phyllis picked up her travelling bag and was about to leave when the ward doors flew open and Inspector Jennings appeared.

'I thought I ordered you away from here!' Adelaide began to protest, but Jennings simply shook his head silently and beckoned for Adelaide to come out into the corridor. When she did so, she was surprised to see her father waiting for her as well. 'What is it?' she asked, hand to mouth. 'Is it Matthew? Or Florence?'

'Nothing like that,' Carlyle assured her. 'But we need you to come outside with us, to the rear exit.'

'Why?' Adelaide demanded as Jennings took her arm to steer her down the hallway.

'There's a dead nurse out there, Adelaide. And we think she may be another of yours.'

8

Adelaide stared, horrified, at the mess. Tangled up with bloodstained discarded surgical cloths, boxes of used implements, towels and used paper in the disposal bin in the rear yard lay the body of a woman in a nurse's uniform, a massive wound visible through the ragged vent in the back of her dark blue gown.

'Is she one of yours?' Jennings asked.

Adelaide shrugged. 'I can't tell without seeing her face. My nurses all wear the standard uniform of the London Hospital nurses, apart from the "Nightingale" name badge that they pin to the front of their tunics.'

Jennings looked across at Carlyle for confirmation. 'May we turn her over?'

Carlyle nodded. 'May as well lift her body out of the bin completely, prior to having her conveyed downstairs to the mortuary.'

On a command from Jennings three constables leaned into the bin and removed the corpse while preserving as much of her dignity as they could maintain. Then they stepped back and Adelaide gave a suppressed squeal of distress.

'It's Edith Crawford,' she squeaked. 'That's to say it *was* her.'

'One of yours?' Jennings asked.

Adelaide nodded. 'Night shift, just like Mary Brennan. She would have left here just after six this morning, but now it's past midday. How come she wasn't spotted earlier?'

'Hard to pick her out among all that refuse and stuff,' Carlyle observed dolefully. 'I'd take a guess that she was killed elsewhere and her body dumped in the rubbish container.'

'Inside the hospital, you mean?' Adelaide asked nervously. 'God forbid!'

'Give me a moment, and everyone else stand to the side,' Carlyle demanded, and the constables joined Jennings alongside the rear wall of the building while Adelaide maintained a lone vigil beside Edith's prone corpse.

Carlyle stared at the ground for a moment, then walked slowly back towards a door set into the rear wall, from which a short flight of two stone steps descended to ground level. 'What's through this door?' he called back to Adelaide.

'It's the nurses' entrance. They come and go through there, then make their way down the side passageway into Whitechapel Road.'

'I thought as much,' Carlyle replied as he walked back to Edith's body and lifted each of her boots in turn, examining their heels intently then summoning Jennings to take a look. 'See these scuff marks on the heels? The nurses obviously keep their boots regularly polished, yet there are clear signs that some of the polish has been scraped off each heel. Then, if you look carefully up the line from the disposal bin that the poor girl was tipped into and towards the nurses' entrance, you'll see the occasional black mark. I'm certain that if you analyse those black marks you'll discover that they're caused by boot polish. Now look at the hem of her skirt — see those dust marks? If you look again along the line formed by those black polish marks, you'll notice that it looks as if someone made a very selective job of sweeping the yard. Your conclusions?'

'She was attacked near the door, then her body was dragged by the armpits along to where she was heaved into the bin.'

'Correct. Further deduction?'

'A man,' Jennings concluded with a confident smile.

Carlyle tapped the side of his nose. 'Beware of settling for the obvious, Inspector. Perhaps two women, acting in concert?'

'You're surely not suggesting her own colleagues?' Adelaide protested. 'My girls would *never* do such a thing — they're dedicated to *saving* lives, not taking them!'

'Nevertheless,' Jennings insisted, 'your father has a valid point. Would the victim have left here alone?'

'Please don't call her "the victim", Inspector,' Adelaide protested. 'Her name was Edith and she was a dedicated nurse, as well as a thoroughly nice young woman. And she no doubt had a family that will be devastated to learn how she came to die. She might even have had a young man.'

'Point taken, but my question remains,' Jennings insisted. 'Would she have been alone when she came out of that door on her way home?'

'I can't be certain, obviously,' Adelaide replied. 'There would have been four of them, Edith, Ellen, Doris and Lily, ending their night duty at the same time, shortly after six a.m. They all live in the same lodging house, so it would be natural for them to leave together. But without speaking to Ellen, Doris and Lily we can't be sure of who left when and whether or not they were all together.'

'I'll obviously need to speak to the other three,' Jennings told her, 'but from what you tell me, they'll be back at the lodging house fast asleep by now.'

'They certainly will, and I'll thank you not to go blundering up there in your size twelve boots to wake them up with such awful news, Inspector,' Adelaide insisted sternly. 'But one thing's obvious from all this, isn't it? It can't be a coincidence that some lunatic is picking off the girls on the night shift, and I must insist that the remaining three be accompanied by police officers on their way to and from work. They live not too far away and they always walk. We might also extend that to the remaining nurses on the day shift, who'll be leaving here at around six this evening, once the night shift girls come back. The shifts are due to change at the end of the week, so that the nurses now on nights revert to days and vice-versa. But the principle remains good — these girls require police protection, if we're to avoid more outrages like this.'

'So you're expecting four police escorts a day?' Jennings asked with a frown.

Adelaide shook her head. 'The girls coming on shift always arrange to be here before the girls who're due to go home finish, otherwise the patients would be left unattended. So what I'm suggesting is that you send, say, two men, who call at the lodging house at around 5.30 in the morning, escort the girls down to work, then bring the off-duty ones back to the lodging house. Then they do the same at around 5.30 in the evening.'

Jennings looked thoughtful before nodding. 'I'll get on to Whitechapel to organise that from Leman Street. I doubt that there'll be any shortage of volunteers for a pleasant roster like that — in fact, the men will probably fight each other for it. You can expect the first lot up at the lodging house by 5.30 this evening, and they'll be strictly instructed to say nothing about why they've been sent until you've had a chance to talk to your nurses.'

'I think it might be better if *you* assure them of their ongoing safety,' Adelaide argued. 'You'll have gathered from what I just told you that for a brief period at around six o'clock this evening you'll have all my nurses on the ward at the same time, so that you can address them all. You'll also then be able to ask whoever shared a room with Edith what she can tell us about

Edith's known movements in her off-duty hours, and Ellen, Doris and Lily can tell you if Edith left here when they did this morning.'

'Sounds like a good idea,' Jennings agreed. 'You might want to bring that husband of yours along too, to give the young ladies some spiritual uplift.'

'He'll need to stay home to look after our daughter, because our childminder leaves for her own home at around five in the evening. Unless, of course, you're prepared to call in at our house sometime this afternoon and ask Matthew to arrange for Mrs Dunning to stay on for an extra hour or two, then bring him back down here.'

'I suppose I could do that,' Jennings agreed reluctantly. 'It would be good to get him involved in all this, I'm thinking, given his ability to soothe the savage breast and pour comfort on disturbed souls.'

'You're beginning to sound as pompous as he does,' Adelaide smirked, 'but I get your point.'

'This is all very interesting,' came Carlyle's voice from alongside the corpse, 'but unless you want me to conduct a post-mortem out here in this rear yard, we need to get the body of this unfortunate young lady down to the mortuary.'

'And I need to get back onto the ward, to let the other girls know what's happened,' Adelaide replied despondently. 'If I had the surgical skills I'd gladly offer to change places with you, Father.'

'And I'd decline,' Carlyle replied kindly. 'Remember that the best leaders are those who only show their true strengths in times of crisis.'

'Then we have to hope that I've got leadership potential, don't we?' Adelaide said as she turned and made her way resignedly towards the rear steps.

It was a gloomy group who gathered around the desk inside the Tower Ward shortly after six o'clock that evening. The nurses from the day shift — Annie Bestwood, Ethel Beamish and Alice Tremayne — had handed over officially to the night shift, whose remaining members, Ellen Tring, Lily Becket, Doris Mooney and the recent arrival Phyllis Collier, had been pleasantly surprised to learn that they had a police escort from the lodging house to work, until advised of the reason for it. Those constables were seated outside the ward while Jennings was conducting a communal interview with all the nurses, obtaining as much information as he could from them regarding Edith Crawford's life, her habits and her last known movements.

She'd shared her room in the lodging house with Annie Bestwood, who'd spent most of the afternoon sniffling into a handkerchief and whimpering quietly to herself. Now she was doing her best to answer the inspector's questions, determined to help all she could with the investigation into her friend's death.

'She came from somewhere in Devon, that's all I really know,' she offered in a wavering voice. 'She grew up on a farm and was determined that she wasn't going to fester away as a farmer's wife, so she came to London hoping to find work in a department store, which she did. Then she became the manageress of a chemist's shop in Islington and took a fancy to medicine. She trained with me in Miss Nightingale's school and we'd been friends for the past five years all told, but I honestly can't think of any possible reason why anyone would want to kill her. It's just … well … all too *horrible!*' She burst into floods of tears and sank heavily to the floor.

Adelaide walked over to comfort her and helped her back to her feet with a pointed stare at Jennings. 'I think she needs a break from all this, Inspector — she's had quite a shock, on top of a busy day on the ward, so please try asking your questions of somebody else.'

'Very well,' Jennings agreed as he cast his eyes round the remaining group. 'I can't remember all your names, I'm afraid, so please remind me which of you finished work when Edith did this morning.'

'Lily, Doris and me, that was all,' Ellen told him. 'We normally all walked back together, particularly after what happened to poor old Mary, attacked while she was walking home alone.'

'And you all left through the nurses' exit at the same time?'

Ellen's face fell. 'No, it was just the three of us — Doris, Lily and me,' she recalled. 'We needed to arrange for more blankets to be delivered to the ward, since these past few nights have got a bit chilly for the patients. I'd normally do that, but I've begun to develop a bit of a head cold, as you can probably tell from the way I'm speaking, so dear Edith volunteered to go and see Matron about it, so that I could get home to bed.' She was on the point of tears as she added, 'If the dear girl hadn't been so thoughtful for my interests, she'd still be alive!'

It was her turn to burst into floods of tears, and Matthew moved from Adelaide's side to lead Ellen gently down the ward and assure her that she had nothing to reproach herself for.

Adelaide watched the two of them idling down the centre of the ward towards the door, then turned on Jennings with a stony stare. 'How many more of my girls do you intend to reduce to tears, Inspector? It's obvious, is it not, that whoever attacked poor Edith took his chance when he saw that she was on her own?'

'We waited for her a few yards down Whitechapel Road,' Lily Becket added sadly. 'Then we decided that Matron had probably kept her talking, and since there was a cold wind blowing we carried on back home. If we'd stayed and waited for her in the side passage, or gone back to look for her, do you think she'd still be alive?'

'Probably not,' Jennings hastened to reassure her. 'Her killer was clearly waiting for the right moment to pounce and seized his opportunity. Even if you'd come straight back into the rear yard, it would have been too late and you'd have been the ones to discover her body.'

'Thank you — I think that's probably enough, Inspector,' Adelaide observed icily. 'It's as if you'd set out to reduce these poor girls to quivering wrecks. Bear in mind that they have patients to minister to.'

'And a damned fine job they make of it, too!' came a man's voice from a nearby bed, and everyone looked round at Major Curran in Bed Three. 'Sorry!' he added in embarrassment, 'but these dear young ladies are the last angels on earth who deserve some filthy coward picking them off like fairground coconuts. That's my opinion, anyway. Take it or leave it.'

'Major Curran,' Adelaide whispered to Jennings. 'He's rather a favourite with the nurses, since he's the least complaining of all our patients. In fact, I'm advised that the girls on the night shift used to take it in turns to sit with him and talk about his days in Egypt with his regiment. And Matthew seems to have got quite friendly with him, since he carries messages backwards and forwards to his wife, who can't always visit on account of the fact that they have two young children.'

'Do you think he might be able to tell us anything of value about what the girls talked about with him?' Jennings asked.

Adelaide shook her head. 'Most of the time he was rambling, particularly in the first week,' she told him. 'Morphine has that effect on you, I'm afraid, and he needed quite a lot of it in the early days. You'd be amazed what patients tell us when they're under the influence.'

'All the same, either of the two murdered girls might have said something to him that the other girls forgot to mention — some link between them that got them killed,' Jennings mused out loud.

Adelaide bristled as she placed her hands on her hips — a gesture that anyone who knew her well would recognise as a warning sign. 'Are you about to suggest that those poor girls were murdered by one of our patients?' she demanded, red-faced. 'As you can see, they're all confined to their beds with horrific injuries, and most of them spend their days floating on clouds of morphine.'

'There are some vacant beds,' Jennings reminded her as he waved both arms to illustrate his point. 'Have you discharged any recently?'

'Only Captain Logan, from Bed Four,' she replied stiffly. 'He was the one who was blinded by the blast, so the least injured. And I may say, between ourselves, that we were thoroughly glad to see the back of him. He was always bemoaning his lot, constantly complaining about the treatment he was receiving and depressing everyone with his gloomy ramblings — *not* morphine-induced, I might add.'

'His attitude also seemed to permeate his family life,' Matthew interjected as he re-joined the group at the desk. 'I attempted to visit him at home to see how he was faring, and his wife informed me that he hadn't shown up there yet. When I spoke to her after the Memorial Service she was very scathing about him too, so I gather that theirs was not a marriage made in Heaven. Which reminds me, Inspector — are you still working on any possible Irish link with the Tower bomb?'

'No, thank God,' Jennings replied. 'I've been taken off that detail to concentrate on these nurse murders, after some idiot tried to suggest that it might be the work of a returning Jack the Ripper. Why do you ask?'

'Probably nothing to it, really, only Logan's wife couldn't resist telling me, while pouring out her venom against him, that he's got a bit of a gambling problem and that his favourite watering hole and card house is a place called "The Shamrock", somewhere in Wapping. You probably know all about the place already, but I thought I'd mention it, since the name suggests an Irish connection.'

'I'll give it some thought,' Jennings promised, 'although I really need to give urgent priority to these murders, before there's another one.'

'Do you think that's likely?' Adelaide asked.

Jennings shrugged. 'As I was quoted as saying in the *Illustrated London News*, I couldn't rule it out. Mind you, that's the only thing the slimy cove quoted me accurately on. But that reminds me of something else I need to ask.' He turned to speak again to Doris and Lily. 'Did you see anyone lurking around near the nurses' exit when you left?'

They both looked blank and shook their heads, but Ellen reminded them, having re-joined the group with reddened eyes, 'There was that coachman, remember?'

'What coachman?' Jennings demanded.

'Well, I took him to be a coachman, anyway. He was standing a few yards away from the exit door, dressed like a coachman, with a long dark cloak and a wide-brimmed hat pulled low over his face. Quite a tall man, I would say, although he was a few feet away, just standing waiting for someone, as I thought at the time.'

'And did you see any coach?'

'No, not now that I think about it. The yard was empty, apart from him.'

'And the coaches normally pull up at the front,' Adelaide told him. 'At least, my father's always does. And no ordinary member of the hospital staff, lowly enough to be required to use the rear exit, would be arriving and departing in a coach. Was that the killer, do you think?'

'It could well have been,' Jennings replied thoughtfully, 'since there was a man answering the same general description hanging around in Brick Lane for a few days before Mary's murder. Ellen, did you recognise the man? Or had you seen him before, anywhere?'

'Not really,' Ellen conceded. 'I only got a passing glimpse of him, and I didn't pay him any heed. We were too busy leaving for home and our beds, chatting away about things in general.'

'The girls from the day shift need to get home,' Adelaide reminded Jennings. 'Let's hope that your constables are still waiting outside for them.'

'I'm sure they will be,' Jennings said, 'and I mustn't disrupt the work of the ward any longer. I'm sorry if I upset some of your more sensitive nurses, but it was important for me to learn as much as I could about the backgrounds of the two who were murdered. In particular, if there was any connection between the two of them. Matthew,' he added in a hushed voice, 'could you make use of your existing good relationship with Major Curran and ask him if the nurses he chatted with said anything that might suggest a connection between them, or some outside relationship that might explain why someone would want to do away with them?'

'*Must* you get my husband involved?' Adelaide demanded in irritation.

Jennings nodded. 'I need all the help I can get, and Matthew has a nice style about him that encourages people to talk freely. Anyway, I must nip downstairs on my way out and see if your father can give me any more information about this second death.'

With that he departed, lifting his hat in farewell to the nurses as he walked towards the double entry doors at the end of the ward.

Ellen smiled at Adelaide as she slipped into the vacant chair behind the desk. 'Time you were going home too, Adelaide. I'll remain with the night shift, if it's alright with you. Even though Phyllis has joined us, the shift's still one short, and if you're happy to make up the numbers on the day shift…'

'Yes, of course,' Adelaide assured her. 'Which reminds me that the shifts are due to change at the weekend, then you'll be back on days, leaving the night shift one short without me. I'll need to give some thought to that.'

'I hope that doesn't mean that you'll be joining the night shift, on which two of the nurses have been murdered already,' Matthew protested.

Adelaide glared back defiantly at him. 'These are *my* nurses and I owe it to them to stand alongside them through these dangerous times.'

'They're not *your* nurses — they're Florence Nightingale's,' Matthew reminded her. 'And you're first and foremost a wife and mother. Don't you think you owe your husband and child some of your devotion as well?'

'He has a point, with the greatest respect,' Ellen added. 'If it would be better for you, I'll stay on nights and we can simply let the remaining nurses change shifts. That way, you can concentrate your efforts on the days; you'll need to be free to contact Miss Nightingale anyway, since we're going to need another replacement.'

'Dear God, I hadn't thought about that,' Adelaide muttered. 'I'm not sure how I can bring myself to tell her.'

'Well, someone has to,' Matthew insisted, 'and you'll need to be at your best when you do that, so you're coming home with me — now. And we're leaving by way of the front entrance, just in case.'

9

Adelaide sighed with irritation as she opened the door to the mortuary and found Jennings already there, talking with her father.

'You seem to spend as much time in this hospital as I do,' she muttered. 'I hope you're not about to spread fear and despondency among my nurses again — you've done enough of that in the press, from what I could see from that copy of the *Illustrated London News* that one of them was reading when she should have been attending to the needs of her patients.'

'I can't be held responsible for the drivel that Buchanan writes,' Jennings growled, 'and I'm here to find out what your father can tell me about Edith Crawford's death.'

'That's why I'm here, as it happens,' Adelaide told him. 'The girls seem to be convinced that Jack the Ripper's back in town.'

'Someone here in the hospital must have tipped off Buchanan about this second death,' Jennings frowned. 'I hope it wasn't one of your nurses, if you tell me that they're so interested in reading the rubbish that Buchanan writes.'

'But *is* it rubbish?' Adelaide countered. 'How can you be sure that the man with the fascination for women's internal organs hasn't decided to renew his self-education?'

'You may not have noticed that I'm here as well,' Carlyle butted in, 'but I've already given Inspector Jennings the benefit of my opinion on why neither of these two nurse murders bore any relationship to those conducted by the man they dubbed "The Ripper".'

'Actually,' Jennings corrected him, 'the man himself awarded himself that name and the gutter press merely fed his vanity by broadcasting it. But as your father has advised me, the Ripper killed his victims by slitting their throats from behind, then removing various organs — very badly, as he advises me. However, whoever killed Mary Brennan and Edith Crawford did so with one blow of a heavy sword, or something similar.'

'He's correct, I'm afraid,' Carlyle confirmed as he looked down at the prone form on his dissection table. 'I don't suppose you want to take a look, Adelaide, but if you were to do so you'd see a deep incision between the shoulder blades that was inflicted with a broad-bladed implement such as a sword. Or perhaps one of those bayonet things.'

'That would have been instantly fatal, I assume?' Adelaide asked as her face lost some of its glow.

Carlyle nodded. 'That's why they issue them to soldiers. I've had little opportunity in the past to study how effective swords are, but this one went in so hard that it actually severed the coronary artery from the *back*.'

'Which raises the interesting question of how someone gained access to military weaponry in a hospital, does it not?' Jennings said.

'Not necessarily,' Adelaide replied. 'Just because poor Edith was murdered at the rear door of a hospital doesn't mean that the weapon came from there, does it? You should surely be conducting enquiries in every military armoury in the country regarding any missing weapons — or would that require you to obtain too much healthy exercise?'

'When the wounded soldiers from the Tower were brought in here,' Jennings enquired of Carlyle, 'do you recall if they were still dressed in their ceremonial uniforms? "Mess Kit", I seem to recall they call it.'

'What you're really asking is whether or not they still had their weapons with them,' Carlyle said, 'and the answer is yes.

We had to unfasten a good deal of leatherwork to get at their wounds and we finished up with a pile of swords, bayonets, rifles and even a pistol.'

'And what did you do with them?'

'Personally, nothing at all, except give instructions that they be removed from where they lay, obstructing vital medical procedures.'

'Instructions to whom?'

'All personal items that come into the hospital with a patient are handed over to the Almoner,' Adelaide told him, 'who's responsible for them until the patient's released.'

'So should I make an enquiry there?' Jennings asked.

Adelaide's face froze.

'The fact remains,' Jennings continued, 'that there were — and hopefully still *are* — various weapons being stored in what is probably a far from secure temporary armoury in here to which any idiot could have had access while masquerading as a soldier. I'm mindful that the description I have of a man seen around the scene of those two murders was tall — perhaps of a military bearing — and more than capable of passing himself off as an Army officer.'

'At least you no longer seem to be accusing any of my nurses,' Adelaide said. 'I can at least give them that reassuring news when I go back onto the ward and advise them that Edith was stabbed in the back and probably wouldn't have felt a thing. But I'll keep quiet about your belief that it might have been a soldier, since they're currently equipped with morphine and might feel inspired to take a revenge of sorts.'

Back on the ward, Adelaide was still getting to know her new day shift of Lily Becket, Doris Mooney and Phyllis Collier that had been in place for less than a week. She decided to leave no-one in any doubt that recent events did not justify any slackness in discipline and walked smartly to the desk at which Phyllis sat reading that morning's *Illustrated London News* and removed it from her hands. She then turned the Ward Report Book round in order to read it and tutted. 'If you paid more attention to patient welfare than rubbish written for credulous imbeciles, then this record would have been brought up to date at least an hour ago. See to it.'

'Yes, Mrs West,' came the crestfallen reply.

Adelaide turned to address the other two. 'Lily, Doris, I strongly recommend that you use this scandal sheet to mop up any spillages, rather than actually reading it. That said, how are you bearing up?'

The two girls assured her that they were fine and Adelaide could only hope that they were being truthful. It was now almost a week since Edith had been cruelly murdered, and the initial shock seemed to have passed; still, there was the reminder, every time they came and went between their lodging house and their work, that two of their number had been slaughtered without warning by a swift, silent assassin armed with a cruel blade wielded without any obvious reason. At least those who had been Edith and Mary's shift companions were now making that journey during the bright light of day and under police escort, but the sadness would remain, along with fear for their night shift equivalents, Ellen Tring, Annie Bestwood, Ethel Beamish and Alice Tremayne.

Since Phyllis seemed to be devoting her assiduous attention to the Ward Report Book, Adelaide decided that she could take a couple of hours off and finally face up to reporting to Florence Nightingale across the river in Lambeth.

As the bus clattered over London Bridge Adelaide began searching for the words, not sure whether Miss Nightingale would already be aware of the murder of another of her skilfully and painstakingly trained nurses and of the need to dispatch another one to what could prove to be an untimely death.

At least the first task had been taken out of her hands. As she walked slowly and fearfully into her presence, Florence rose from behind her desk and moved round it to take Adelaide comfortingly by the arm and lower her into the visitor's chair, prior to ringing her little desk bell and ordering tea and cakes for two. Then she resumed her seat behind the other side of the desk and smiled kindly at Adelaide. 'My poor child — what did I commit you to? How are my other nurses bearing up?'

'Fine, now,' Adelaide replied, grateful that the worst purpose for her journey had already been achieved without any effort on her part. 'They were obviously deeply shocked and in the main somewhat tearful, but they've rallied round and are to be commended for putting the interests of the patients first, as usual.'

'Why would anyone wish to slaughter my dedicated young ladies?' Florence asked, seemingly of the ceiling.

Adelaide had prepared her answer. 'It has to be hoped that the killings were random. What I mean by that is that although it was tragic that two of our nurses coincidentally became victims of the same lunatic, it was simply the case that they were in the wrong place at the wrong time and *not* the case that some maniac has a homicidal attraction to our nurses. So far as the police have been able to determine, there was no connection between the two other than the fact that they worked alongside each other on the same shift.'

'You're certain of that?'

'Not me, the Scotland Yard inspector in charge.'

'And has your husband been able to comfort the remaining girls?'

'Not as much as perhaps he'd like. He has his own parish duties to attend to, as well as ensuring that our daughter is being properly fed and otherwise looked after.'

'But he's been of some assistance?'

'To me, certainly, by his very presence. But curiously he's also been able to form trusting relationships with most of our patients — and one in particular — and that seems to raise their spirits as much as good and attentive nursing.'

'Speaking of which, you presumably require a replacement for this latest one to be killed?'

'If possible, but I'm also conscious of the danger to anyone dressed as a nurse at the London Hospital at present. It continues to be the case that we can cope with one missing, bearing in mind the generously low patient numbers that we began with, the fact that we'd got used to reduced numbers before Edith's death and of course the addition of Phyllis Collier, who's settling in well, by the way.'

'That's probably all to the good,' Florence frowned, 'since the trustees of my nursing trust have left me in no doubt that they don't wish to see any more young ladies dispatched to the London Hospital during the current — "situation", shall we call it?'

Matthew heard the knocking on the front door above Florrie's squeals of protest as she jerked her head from side to side in order to avoid what Violet Dunning was attempting to get her to eat, which to Matthew looked like some sort of large dog biscuit.

He sighed and opened the door, to reveal the awkward-looking presence of the vicar, Joseph Mulholland.

'Sorry to disturb your breakfast, Matthew,' he mumbled, 'but I wonder if I might step inside for a moment?'

Matthew showed him into the sitting room, where Joseph seated himself, as invited, in the armchair and immediately grabbed his pocket handkerchief as he began sneezing. Once the attack was over, he looked up pleadingly at Matthew.

'As you can see, I've got a nasty dose of something and the doctor's confined me to the house for a few days. The problem is that I'm under considerable pressure from that dreadful Colonel from the Coldstreamers to increase my pastoral visits to the wives and widows at the Tower Barracks, and I was wondering if I could trade on your good nature to substitute for me. I know that you've done a couple of visits there already, so you'll know most of the ladies concerned.'

'I have indeed,' Matthew confirmed with a smile, 'and one in particular — the wife of Major Curran, for whom I carry messages back and forth from her husband, who's still in a hospital bed, but who we hope will be discharged in the near future. I can begin with her and see who else needs our comforting presence and perhaps some appropriate passages from the Bible.'

'I knew I could count on you, and I'll be forever grateful,' Mulholland managed to respond before another bout of sneezing overtook him and he departed, face in his soggy handkerchief.

Two hours later, Matthew strolled into the courtyard of the Waterloo Barracks, where the first thing that met his eye was Rose Curran, hanging washing out on the communal lines that ran down the entire length of the wall that separated the officers' living quarters from the parade square. She smiled nervously as she saw him approaching, then called out,

'Everything alright with Tom?'

'Yes, indeed,' Matthew reassured her. 'I'm here in place of Reverend Mulholland, making his regular visit for him because he has a heavy cold.'

'Come in anyway and I'll make us a mug of tea,' Rose said, 'and this time I already have cake, so no polite refusal.'

A few minutes later Matthew was seated in the cramped living room and Rose was telling him all about the latest antics of her two children. 'They tend to play by themselves and of course we're stuck inside the Tower complex, so they can't play in the street like other kids.'

'It must be very restrictive, but don't you get moved around from place to place?' Matthew asked.

Rose shrugged. 'That's what we were promised, and it's obviously better than having Tom away in Egypt or wherever, but we've been stuck here for months now. I think we were due to move back to Aldershot, although that's almost as bad. But of course it won't be happening, now that Tom only has one arm and we'll all be moving to Reading. At least the kids will have somewhere to run around and burn off some energy.'

'There are no other children of the same age around here?' Matthew asked.

Rose shook her head. 'Not really. There's Olive Hargraves next door at Number 9 and she's got a son aged thirteen or so, who's only interested in following his dad into the regiment, although maybe he's changed his tune since his father lost half his leg. Then down in Number 7 you'll find Jim Owen's wife Clara, and they don't have any kids. Number 5's that dreadful Logan woman and her noisy brats, but I wouldn't want my two associating with them.'

'I came across Mary Logan during my last visit,' Matthew said diplomatically.

Rose snorted quietly into her tea. 'I hope she didn't invite you in, what with you being a vicar and all, because it wouldn't have done your reputation any good.'

'In what way?' Matthew asked politely, although he anticipated the answer that followed.

'Between you and me, she's no better than she should be, as they say, although in her case she's worse. There's men going in and out of her place at all hours of the day and night and she's got no shame — doesn't even try to hide it from the others in the row. And it's not just since her husband finished up in the hospital, either — she was at it long before then, and they used to have blazing arguments about it that the entire row could hear. He has an addiction to gambling, you see, and she claims that she needs to entertain "gentlemen friends" to make ends meet, but the truth is that she enjoys the — well, you know, *that* sort of thing.'

'Has her husband returned home yet?'

'I wasn't aware that he was out of hospital, but no, we haven't seen him around here for weeks. And believe me, we'd all know if he was back home, because the screaming matches would have started up again.'

'She did mention that he might be staying in some hostelry in Wapping that he likes to frequent,' Matthew added diplomatically, earning himself another snort from Rose.

'A "hostelry" — was that her word for it? It's a common whorehouse, if you mean "The Shamrock". The men have all been warned off it, and I heard tell that any officer caught in there will be cashiered out of the regiment. Is that where Logan's skulking?'

'That was what his wife suggested, certainly. But why has the regiment declared it off-limits?'

'There's meant to be some sort of unhealthy Irish connection, but that's only rumour, of course. The real reason is probably that they don't want the men, and particularly the officers, catching some dreadful disease from the trollops in there, or running up debts playing cards. But since that dreadful explosion that the Fenians are being blamed for, the bad feeling against the Irish has got a lot worse around here, as you'll no doubt appreciate.'

'Yes indeed,' Matthew agreed. 'I did actually advise a police officer of my acquaintance that there might be some Irish connection in The Shamrock, given its name, but I'm not sure if he's followed up on it.'

'Well, God help Gerard Logan if he's found in there, that's all. Oh, sorry, didn't mean to blaspheme or anything.'

'Think no more of it, Mrs Curran, since I hear it five times a day in the course of my work. Which reminds me of why I'm really here. Do you happen to know of any other regimental wives who're likely to be in particular need of spiritual comfort at this time?'

Rose thought for a moment before replying. 'The widows have been particularly devastated, as you'd expect. Poor old Lydia Mullens moved out of Number 1 and went back to her family in Lincolnshire somewhere, but there's Marjory Kelly next door at Number 13, who I hear crying through the wall most nights. She's expecting again and not far from her time, so she might welcome a visit from you. And if you want any more information about The Shamrock, ask Tom.'

Promising to take up both of her suggestions and after thanking her for the tea and cake, Matthew took his leave and knocked apprehensively on the door of Number 13, praying to God to give him the words he needed to comfort a pregnant widow.

Phyllis Collier paced impatiently up and down the kitchen of the lodging house, while Doris Mooney went outside to assure the waiting constables that they wouldn't be much longer. She came back in with a smile. 'That tall one with the blue eyes is quite a charmer, isn't he? Isn't Lily down yet? We need to get a move on if we're to avoid a dressing down from Adelaide West.'

The three of them were assembling prior to being escorted down to the London Hospital for their day shift by their regular police guard, two young constables who were smoking their pipes in the passageway outside as they waited for them. Phyllis had already knocked on Lily's door twice, receiving no reply, and she suspected that the girl was still fast asleep. Rather than set off without her, leaving her to hurry down to work late and without any police protection, Phyllis opted to walk down the ground-floor corridor to the rooms occupied by the lodging superintendent, Mrs Huggins, to ask her to open Lily's door with her master key, in the belief that it would be locked.

A very disgruntled and dishevelled Mrs Huggins simply handed Phyllis the key and told her to bring it back when she'd finished with it. Phyllis told Doris to wait for her outside while she roused Lily, then set off upstairs. Doris did as instructed and was busily engaged in making eyes at Constable Beresford when a series of piercing screams ripped through the lodging house and out into the alleyway, sending the two constables racing inside.

10

James Carlyle looked down briefly at the sobbing girl draped across the kitchen table in the lodging house before making his way upstairs, where a uniformed constable indicated with a brief nod that the room he was seeking was just to the left. He walked in and addressed the back of Inspector Jennings as he hunched over what was lying in the bed. 'I came as quickly as I could,' Carlyle told him. 'Another nurse, I understand.'

Jennings growled his confirmation. 'This one's called Lily Becket — or rather, she *was*, before someone came calling. The attack looks like the other two.'

'With at least one important difference, Inspector. This one was indoors.'

'Indeed, and look what a mess he left for us.'

Jennings stood aside and Carlyle peered down at the corpse: a young woman in her mid-twenties, still dressed in the remains of a plain white nightgown that had presumably not originally been designed with a gaping hole in the front, through which blood could splatter out in all directions. He looked down quickly to its hem, which lay completely undisturbed, and temporarily ruled out any sort of sexual motive, although the further tests he would conduct in the mortuary would confirm that point.

Then on a whim he looked at the wall adjoining the bed, then up at the ceiling. Fine sprays of something that had already dried to a mid-brown colour confirmed his initial suspicion that the fatal blow had been to the heart, with a resulting initial fountain of lifeblood before it stopped pumping.

'Whoever did this will be covered in blood,' he told Jennings. 'If it happened during the night, then the chances are that he slipped away without being noticed and has since had the opportunity to wash or burn his clothes.' Carlyle placed the back of his hand on the corpse's forehead and thought briefly. 'She's still slightly warm, so probably no more than a few hours at most. It's nine a.m. now, so let's say four or five this morning.'

'Still doesn't help me,' Jennings said. 'He could be anywhere by now. I take it that she *was* stabbed through the heart with a sword or something? I'm no doctor, obviously, but even I can see that.'

'Correct, on provisional diagnosis,' Carlyle confirmed. 'And from the way she's lying, she was fast asleep at the time, so knew nothing about it.'

'That's some blessing at least,' Jennings conceded. 'So she wouldn't have been able to put up a fight?'

Carlyle sighed heavily. 'A young slip of a girl against a hulking brute armed with a sword — what do *you* think? Even less if she was asleep until the last second. But let's just check, shall we?' He lifted up both the victim's hands and looked carefully at, and under, the fingernails. 'Nothing suggestive of a fight, anyway. I'd take a guess that she was in a deep sleep at the time, so as not to have heard the door being forced.'

'You're not getting all the forensic glory, doctor. I already examined the doorframe, and there's no sign of it being forced. Added to which the girl who found her assures us that the door was unlocked.'

'Is that the one down in the kitchen, sobbing her heart out?'

'That's her. Name of Phyllis Collier. A colleague of the dead girl who's asked that word be taken to Adelaide of what's happened. There's another one too, a girl called Doris Mooney, and we'll let her go once we've got as much as we can out of her. The Collier girl may need sedation.'

'Why would a girl like this leave her room door unlocked, given the fate that recently befell two of her colleagues?' Carlyle mused out loud.

Jennings gave a polite cough before suggesting, 'Perhaps she left it open for a young man? Or even an older man? These girls share a room, but only in the sense that one works while the other sleeps. This one — Lily Becket — would have had the room to herself.'

'Didn't the lodging house superintendent have a policy against that sort of thing?' Carlyle asked. 'What's his name, anyway, since I'll presumably need to speak to him?'

'It's a woman — a Mrs Huggins. There's no Mr Huggins, apparently, and unless my nose is playing tricks…' Jennings mimicked the motion of someone taking a long slug direct from a bottle, and Carlyle decided against attempting to speak to the lady in question regarding the moral habits of her tenants.

'You can remove the body down to the mortuary whenever you like,' Carlyle announced, 'and I assume that you'll be pursuing the thankless process of conducting enquiries locally regarding whether or not anyone happened to see a tall man in a cloak and a wide-brimmed hat staggering down the street in the early hours, covered in blood. Then again, given the locality, that's perhaps not such an unlikely sight.'

'I thought only we bobbies were that cynical,' Jennings said as he signalled for the body to be taken downstairs to the waiting wagon.

'Spend a week in my mortuary and try to maintain any residual faith in human nature,' Carlyle replied as he stepped out of the room and hurried down the stairs to speak with

Doris Mooney in an effort to delay her journey to the hospital. To which he'd need to take himself off without delay, he realised. Sometimes a girl needed a father, and this was one of those times.

Adelaide reached for the fob watch that was suspended by a chain around her neck, consulted it for the fourth time that morning and clucked her annoyance. It was now shortly after ten in the morning; the exhausted night shift nurses were drooping with fatigue and there was no sign of the day shift.

Something must have gone seriously wrong for the girls not to have shown up at all. If only two of them had arrived, bearing excuses for the third, that would have been bad enough, but for all three to fail to report for duty suggested something far more ominous. She was therefore hardly surprised when the ward doors opened and there stood Matron Beswick, a serious expression on her face as she beckoned Adelaide to the door with an imperious wave of her hand. Whispering to Ellen that she wouldn't be long and that the nightshift would soon be able to go home for some much-needed sleep, Adelaide followed at Matron's heels, along the corridor and down a flight of stairs towards Matron's room on the ground floor.

'I'm sorry the shifts haven't changed yet,' she called breathlessly as she scuttled along behind the formidable bulk of the much-feared harridan who ruled the nursing staff with a rod of iron, 'but I was about to send someone to find out what's holding them back.'

Matron remained silent until they reached her office. The first thing to catch Adelaide's eye was her father, sitting solemnly behind a tray of teacups and a pot of tea. Adelaide looked enquiringly at Matron, who waved her into a seat with a brusque, 'Your father will explain, but first help yourself to a cup of tea.'

'I've already poured you one,' Carlyle responded as he pushed a cup towards her.

At a loss to understand what this was all about, but suddenly experiencing a dry throat, Adelaide did as requested, downing the entire cup in three swallows as she awaited an explanation. Finally, her father broke the silence.

'I'm afraid you're going to be two short on your day shift,' he told her, then awaited her reply.

'*None* of the girls have turned up yet, and it's after ten,' Adelaide replied. 'I was about to send someone to their lodging house.'

'I've just come from there — in my professional capacity,' Carlyle replied as gently as he could.

Adelaide's hand flew to her mouth. '*Two*? Dear God, no — don't tell me that *two more* of them have been murdered!'

'No, only one,' Carlyle reassured her. 'Lily Becket. But Phyllis Collier's under sedation, since she was the one who found the body. Doris Mooney promised to get here by dinner time, although she's badly shaken.'

'Don't worry, my dear,' Matron Beswick assured her in the softest tone Adelaide had ever heard her employ, 'I can let you have replacements from the other wards.'

'So what? How? When?' Adelaide demanded as she tried to get her fuzzy thoughts into some sort of logical sequence. It was her father who supplied the answer.

'It seems that someone entered her room while she was asleep. She'd foolishly left the door unlocked, for reasons which Inspector Jennings is still investigating, and if it's any consolation it happened while she was asleep.'

'The same as Mary and Edith? A blow with a sword?'

'So it would seem.'

Adelaide's head felt as if it was wrapped in heavy blankets and she struggled to find something to say, marvelling at the fact that she wasn't screaming the room down. She looked stupidly across at Matron Beswick with what, in any other circumstances, would have seemed like an unfeeling question, bearing in mind what had just happened. 'You're sure you can find suitable replacements?' she asked.

'Miss Nightingale isn't the only one who trains nurses, and I can spare two from the General Ward for the time being. You already had a somewhat generous caseload in your Tower Ward by my standards, and two of those have already been discharged, leaving you with only four. Most of my nurses would be expected to handle that number and perhaps more on their own, so you can let your night shift girls go home with a clear conscience. My two will hold the fort until the one you're expecting turns up, and I'll ensure that the Ward Report by which Miss Nightingale seems to set such store is filled in regularly.'

'That's my job,' Adelaide insisted.

Her father shook his head. 'You'll be in no condition, and I've sent word to Matthew to come and escort you home in my coach.'

'What do you mean, in no condition?' Adelaide demanded. 'I'll admit that I'm feeling a bit fuzzy-headed right at this moment, but that's no doubt the shock.'

'Within half an hour you'll be nodding off,' Carlyle assured her and when Adelaide raised both eyebrows in defiant question, he pointed to her teacup with a wry smile. 'Laudanum,' he told her.

Adelaide stared at Matron in disbelief. 'You allowed him to lace my tea with laudanum?'

Matron nodded. 'You'll thank us both when you wake up later today at home and take it all in. But for the time being, you're in no condition to be in charge of a ward full of patients.'

Adelaide was about to protest when the office door burst open and there stood Matthew.

'What's happened?' he demanded, worry creasing his face. 'I got word to come and get you from the hospital — has something happened? Are you ill?'

'Lily Becket's been murdered,' she told him flatly.

Matthew looked enquiringly at Carlyle. 'Here at the hospital?'

Carlyle shook his head. 'No, at her lodgings. But it was necessary to sedate Adelaide, so you need to take her home before the medication takes full effect.'

'It *wasn't* necessary to sedate me,' Adelaide protested as Matthew took her arm and eased her out of her chair.

'Don't argue with a doctor who also happens to be your father,' Matthew said as she offered no resistance, then he looked back at Carlyle. 'Will she suffer any ill effects from what you gave her?'

Carlyle shook his head with a smile. 'If laudanum were poison, half the children in the East End would be motherless. She'll sleep for a few hours, I imagine, but if she starts seeing little green men on her bedside table, call for me.'

Inspector Jennings left the almoner in little doubt of what he thought of his security arrangements. 'Anyone could walk in here, pretending to be one of those Guards officers, and walk out with enough weaponry to take on half a dozen of my bobbies.'

'As I understand it, your bobbies have been demanding for some time that they be armed with something better than billy clubs,' the almoner replied coldly, 'so perhaps you might want to raise the matter with your police commissioner. As for my security arrangements, they're normally sufficient for personal adornments such as fob watches, hats, walking sticks and the occasional set of artificial teeth. Since we rarely get swords and pistols, we took extreme care over those items when they were dumped in here, without, I might add, any attempt to indicate who they belonged to. But I was able to obtain, from someone at the Tower, a reliable list of what each of the officers would have been issued with and wearing at the time of the explosion. And if you consult my record here, you'll see that two of the officers have already been discharged with what they were entitled to. I cannot, of course, guarantee that they each got back the very items that they came in with, but at least they didn't walk out of her with something to which they were not entitled.'

Jennings had been studying the record book while the almoner had been prattling on, and he made a note in his own notebook that Captain John Sweeney had been the first to be discharged, followed by Captain Gerard Logan a few days later. Each had received a bayonet and sword, but nothing else.

Thanking him coldly for his assistance, Jennings made a short trip down to the mortuary to receive confirmation that the latest victim had died in the same way as the others. Then, after visiting the Tower Ward in order to speak with Doris

Mooney, he headed back to Scotland Yard for a meeting with the Irish Branch in the hope that they could provide him with some light down the long dark tunnel that this investigation had become.

Adelaide turned over sleepily and found herself looking into Matthew's eyes as he stared down at her with concern. Then she realised that he was illuminated, not in a halo glow as her befuddled brain had first imagined, but in the light from the bedside lamp.

'What time is it?' she asked as she slowly came awake.

'I'm not telling you, if it means that you'll try to get up and go down to that damned hospital,' Matthew replied in a voice laced with determination.

'That "damned hospital", as you call it, has several sick patients who're my responsibility,' Adelaide reminded him. 'Did Mrs Dunning leave anything for tea? I'm starving.'

'Hungry enough to eat something that I've made?' Matthew asked and when Adelaide pulled a face, he laughed and added, 'With a little assistance from one of your nurses.'

'Who?' she demanded.

'Doris Mooney. She's staying with us for a while, if that's in order. Only she's too scared to go back to that lodging house where ... well, anyway, a police officer brought her here with a request from Inspector Jennings that we give her sanctuary. As a man of God I could hardly refuse, but the bonus is that Doris used to be a cook in a hotel in Northampton before she heard the call of Nightingales, and she's helped me put together a very promising-smelling meat pie. That's why I came to wake you up. And in answer to your original question, it's just coming on eight o'clock in the evening, and you're not the only one who's hungry.'

'I can't believe that my own father drugged me,' Adelaide muttered as she climbed into some clothes and threw her nightdress into the washing basket in the corner.

'Would you rather that it had been someone else's father?' Matthew joked, and Adelaide pulled a face.

Downstairs the table had been set, and a delicious aroma of hot meaty pastry filled the kitchen that also served as a dining room.

'Are you sure you don't mind, Mrs West?' Doris asked bashfully. 'Only your husband said it would be in order, and I really don't think I could bring myself to...' She broke off.

Adelaide smiled warmly. 'I won't mind, provided that you call me Adelaide and my husband Matthew. But if this pie doesn't live up to its delicious smell, I may have to reconsider the arrangement. I hope you kept careful watch over what Matthew was doing.'

Assuring her that she had, Doris turned back to the sink, straining first the potatoes, then the carrots into dishes before placing them both on the table and taking the remaining seat. Matthew said Grace, then they all helped themselves with appreciative murmurs.

'I'm sure that Matthew will disapprove of my talking about work,' Adelaide said between mouthfuls, 'but did you manage to get to the hospital today? And if so, are they managing?'

'Quite well,' Doris reassured her. 'Matron Beswick sent two others along — mainly to spy on us, I think — and they were over the moon to have only one patient each. Ellen should be back tomorrow, and of course the night shift will come back on as normal, since the three who died were all from the same day shift. Mine, of course, which is why I'm terrified that I'll be next.'

114

'Do you know of any reason why the dead girls all came from the same shift?' Matthew asked, despite a warning glare from Adelaide. 'Isn't it all just an unfortunate coincidence — the work of a random maniac with a "down" on nurses — or do you have reason to believe that your shift has been singled out for a reason?'

'None, really, except that Inspector Jennings suggested that it was a possibility. He came onto the ward early this afternoon, asking lots of questions about poor Lily's private life, but in fact I don't believe she had one. I began crying, I'm afraid, and blurted out how fearful I was about going back to that lodging house. It was then that the inspector arranged for his coach to bring me up here, with an assurance that I'd be welcome.'

'He left a note of sorts,' Matthew added for Adelaide's benefit, 'and don't be surprised if we see his face up here sometime this evening, so perhaps it would be better that we help ourselves to seconds before he does.'

They were in fact enjoying a pot of tea by the time the knock on the door came and Matthew got up to answer it.

Jennings came into the sitting room and had just made a point of asking Doris if she'd settled in when Adelaide cut in on him.

'As it transpires, we've just enjoyed one of the best meals I've had in ages, Inspector, so Doris is a most acceptable house guest, but the next time you have in mind inviting someone to stay with us, you might consult either my husband or myself first.'

'Point taken,' Jennings conceded, 'but there was a purpose behind it.'

'Clearly you believe that Doris may still be at risk,' Matthew concluded, 'but isn't that true of the other nurses living in that lodging house? The entire night shift, for one thing — what are you doing to preserve them from this lunatic?'

'That's why I'm here,' Jennings replied as he took a seat without invitation and was grudgingly offered a cup of tea. 'I think that the time has come for us all to get our thinking caps on and work out what this loony's about, because I don't think it's random and I have a gut feeling that it's also linked with that Tower bomb in some way.'

'What way?' Matthew asked.

Jennings smiled. 'That's why we're all here in the one place at the same time. I think that between us we can begin to complete a jigsaw puzzle. I suggest that we begin with what we know already. That is, those facts that can't be controverted. The first is the bomb explosion inside the Tower Barracks on the 18th of June, some six weeks ago now. That led to the admission of eight Guards officers into a special ward designated by Doctor Carlyle, which became six after two of them succumbed to their injuries.'

'This belief of yours that the murders are connected with the Tower bombing, isn't that just an assumption on your part?' Matthew asked.

'It is,' Jennings conceded, 'but in my business you learn that so-called coincidences are sometimes far from being coincidences. Who have been the three victims of the recent murders?'

'I think you've made your point there, Inspector,' Adelaide commented with a sideways look at Matthew. 'The nurses who died were all ministering to survivors of that bomb.'

'And all from the same group,' Doris added quietly. 'When the eight of us were first sent by Miss Nightingale to staff the Tower Ward, we divided ourselves into two groups of four. There were Ellen, Annie, Ethel and Alice in one group and

Mary, Edith, Lily and myself in the other. We were joined by Ellen after Mary was murdered, but she wasn't in that original group of four, of which I'm the only survivor. That makes me very frightened, I have to admit.'

'We'll get back to the future arrangements for your safety in a moment,' Jennings promised her. 'Let's remind ourselves of other considerations that we need to take into account.'

'Such as?' Matthew asked.

Jennings continued. 'The murders have all been inflicted with a sword, bayonet or other military-style weapon, according to Carlyle. I'm inclined towards the use of a bayonet, since it would be more easily concealed beneath the cloak of the man seen in the vicinity of the first two murders. The man prowling Brick Lane in the case of Mary's murder and the man that Ellen Tring took to be a coachman on the morning that Edith was killed.'

'But only Ellen saw him,' Doris reminded them.

'Just because you others didn't see him doesn't mean that he wasn't there. If it comes to that, no-one yet has reported seeing anyone lurking around the lodging house on the night of this latest murder of Lily. But we can't ignore the alleged coincidence of the sighting of what sounds like the same man at the scene of two of those murders, because so far as I'm aware Ellen knew nothing of the description of the suspect that I'd received during my investigation in Brick Lane. You understand the point I'm making?' Heartened by the fact that no-one saw fit to argue with him, Jennings continued. 'That description would fit a Guards officer, would it not?'

'Surely not one of our patients?' Doris objected. 'They were all confined to their sickbeds, and all but two of them were recovering from amputations.'

'Not all of them, by the date of the first murder — Mary's,' Jennings reminded them. 'By the time that Mary was attacked in Brick Lane, two of your patients had recently been discharged, had they not? At least, that's what your Ward Report book shows, and I have every faith in Adelaide's competence and conscientiousness in that regard.'

'As indeed you should,' Adelaide said appreciatively.

Doris thought back briefly before announcing, 'Captain Sweeney and Captain Logan.'

'Precisely,' Jennings concurred. 'I checked with the hospital almoner and both men were discharged with the weapons they'd had in their possession when first admitted as patients. In the case of Captain Sweeney, his young lady brought him a selection of fresh civilian clothes, because his dress uniform was horribly bloodstained from his chest injuries, but the almoner distinctly remembers Captain Logan being dressed in his officer's Mess uniform when he called to collect his sword and bayonet.'

'But no-one's reported any sighting of a man dressed as a soldier at the scenes of the two murders,' Matthew pointed out, earning himself an annoyed frown from Jennings.

'I'm not suggesting that Captain Logan, or anyone else, committed the murders dressed in anything resembling a distinctive army uniform,' he muttered. 'That would be far too obvious to any eye-witnesses at the scene. I'm merely pointing out that before the murders began, two of the former patients in the Tower Ward were discharged in possession of weapons that could have been used to murder those poor unfortunate girls.'

'By the same token,' Matthew argued back, '*any* deranged soldier — from *any* regiment — could legitimately gain access to a weapon such as that. If it comes to that, such a weapon could easily have been stolen.'

'Really?' Jennings asked. 'From the armoury inside the Tower of London?'

'From *any* armoury,' Matthew persisted. 'Or, if it comes to that, from the almoner's office inside the hospital.'

'I already checked,' Jennings replied. 'I examined the almoner's records, as well as conducting a physical stock-take myself, and no weapons have left the almoner's office other than those checked out to Captains Sweeney and Logan.'

'So was it one of them, is that what you're saying?' Adelaide asked.

Jennings shrugged his response. 'I'm just saying that they are possible suspects, on the basis of the facts that we currently have to hand.'

'Surely not Captain Sweeney?' Doris objected. 'He was such a nice man and such an uncomplaining patient.'

'Doris is right,' Adelaide confirmed. 'He has a fiancée who visited him in the ward, and they're planning on getting married sometime later this year. He's the last person of all of them that I'd suspect of being capable of the sort of savagery that Mary, Lily and Edith suffered. Sorry, Doris, that probably doesn't make you feel any easier in your mind.'

'It makes me more prepared to believe that it might have been Captain Logan, though,' Doris grimaced. 'He was the very opposite of Captain Sweeney — always complaining, always feeling sorry for himself, never taking comfort from the fact that he hadn't lost an arm or a leg.'

'And a thoroughly degenerate character, according to even his own wife,' Matthew added, 'not to mention his close neighbour in the officers' living quarters, Mrs Curran. She had no hesitation in telling me what dreadful people they both are, him with a gambling addiction, spending nights away from home, and her "entertaining" gentlemen for money.'

'That doesn't make him a murderer, though,' Adelaide pointed out.

It fell silent until Doris suddenly opened up again. 'Talking about the patients has just reminded me of something that I'd forgotten all about until now. It may not be important, but since we're adding in everything we know, perhaps I should mention it.'

'Go on,' Jennings invited her.

'In the first week or two, before Mary was murdered and Ellen joined us, we used to spend a lot of time at Captain Curran's bedside during the night shift, making sure that he had enough morphine. We felt so sorry for him, and he was so brave and we may have overdone the medications occasionally — sorry, Adelaide.'

'Keep going,' Jennings urged her impatiently.

'Well, sometimes he'd begin talking in his — his "sleep", I suppose you'd call it. He seemed to be drifting back to the explosion itself, and he kept mentioning Captain Logan's eyes. He was concerned that a fellow officer had lost his eyesight, or so we thought, but there was one night when Captain Logan, who was in the adjoining bed and who we thought had been asleep himself, got very excited and angry, telling Captain Curran to shut his mouth, or he'd shut it for him. He'd obviously heard what we all had and was clearly displeased.'

'Why would someone be displeased that a friend and colleague was concerned regarding his lost eyesight?' Matthew mused.

Jennings's face had lit up. 'Carlyle mentioned in passing that there was something unusual — something he couldn't fathom — about why Logan had survived with only flash burns to his face. If Curran was making the same point and Logan wanted to silence him, then perhaps there's something in it that connects back to the explosion itself.'

'But why would that lead to three nurses being murdered?' Adelaide questioned.

Doris added, 'And why murder Mary and Edith, when so far as I can remember it was only Lily and myself who were sitting with Captain Curran on the night that Captain Logan yelled at him? I'd just given Captain Curran some more morphine and Lily was mopping his forehead and holding his hand, urging him not to upset himself.'

'I know why!' Jennings said suddenly, causing the others to start slightly. 'Think back to Logan's injuries — flash burns to the face, yes?'

'Yes,' Doris confirmed, 'but that wouldn't have affected his hearing.'

'Not his hearing — his eyesight!' Adelaide pointed out excitedly, as the realisation dawned.

Jennings nodded eagerly. 'Precisely! His face — and particularly his eyes — were bandaged over, were they not?'

'Yes, those were Doctor Carlyle's instructions, and the bandages didn't come off until the day before he was discharged,' Doris confirmed. 'But I still don't see what —'

'He couldn't see!' Jennings exclaimed. 'He knew that there were nurses at Curran's bedside, but he didn't know which ones they were because his eyes were bandaged. All he knew was that they were nurses on duty at the time. This was on the night shift, you said?'

'Yes — but…'

'Doris,' Adelaide pointed out. 'What Inspector Jennings is trying to break to you gently is that because he didn't know which of the nurses on duty had heard what Curran was saying, he had to murder *all* of them!'

'Including me?' Doris asked.

Jennings confirmed, 'Including you,' and Doris sat staring into the distance.

'Was there ever a time when Logan could have found out which of the nurses it could have been?' Matthew asked, still not convinced.

Doris's eyes opened wide as the memory came back to her. 'Yes, there was! The final night that he was on the ward. Doctor Carlyle had removed the bandages that morning and told Captain Logan that he could go home after one more night on the ward, allowing his eyes time to focus. We thought it out of character at the time, when Captain Logan sat up in bed and insisted on thanking each of his nurses, one after the other, for all the kindness we'd shown him. He did the same with the day shift, apparently, and he'd have been able to memorise our names and what each of us looked like.'

'From what you tell me, you aren't the only one who's still in danger,' Jennings said. 'If there's one person above all who Logan wants dead, it's Captain Curran.'

'He's still on the ward,' Adelaide pointed out, 'and surely Logan wouldn't try anything in full view of several nurses?'

'But Curran's due for discharge in a few days, or so we were told,' Doris told them.

Jennings sat deep in thought before issuing instructions as if to his own constables. 'He clearly can't be allowed to leave while he's in such danger, and I'll impress that point on Carlyle. I'll also need to speak to him, and preferably in private.' He turned to Adelaide. 'Is it possible to put him in some sort of ward all on his own?'

'The hospital has isolation wards, certainly,' Adelaide confirmed, 'although they're just for patients who're infectious.'

'It surely wouldn't be challenged by anyone if your father had him committed into isolation, would it?'

'Of course not,' Adelaide said. 'Father's regarded as little short of God by Matron, and she'd be in no position to challenge his medical judgment.'

'But why do you need to keep him isolated while you question him?' Matthew asked. 'If you're right and Logan's the murderer and he's been discharged, then surely he doesn't pose any danger to those on the ward and won't be around to hear whatever Captain Curran can tell you?'

'If I'm right and if the murders have been committed in order to cover up Logan's involvement in the explosion, then he might not be the only one on that ward to have been involved. Presumably if one person says something inside that relatively small and purposely quiet room, everyone can hear it?'

'That's true,' Adelaide confirmed, 'but are you suggesting that someone still left on the ward was so determined to assist in causing an explosion that they deliberately sat there while it went off, risking the loss of a limb?'

'Don't underestimate the insane determination of the Fenians,' Jennings muttered. 'He wouldn't be the first to get himself killed while detonating a bomb. Three of them died trying to blow up London Bridge some ten years ago. As for Logan himself, he was sitting at the extreme right-hand end of the table, which was why he came off relatively lightly.'

'A man that deranged wouldn't think twice about murdering three nurses in cold blood,' Matthew observed and Doris gasped. Adelaide gave Matthew a hard stare and shook her head in disapproval as Jennings sought to repair the damage.

'Our first priority must be to ensure that he doesn't succeed in murdering a fourth. Adelaide, may I take it that you'd be prepared to allow Doris to extend her stay here?'

'Of course.'

'And she's now on the day shift, along with you?'

'Yes, except I'm not there all the time. I have to report to Miss Nightingale on a regular basis, and whenever possible I like to slip back home to spend time with our daughter.'

'Once Doris gets to work she'll be safe enough on the ward, I think,' Jennings replied as he thought through the necessary arrangements. 'How do you travel to and from the hospital each day, Adelaide?'

'The bus that takes me down Mile End Road and onto Whitechapel Road. It's only a few stops down the road, but I have to walk up Stepney Green or White Horse Road to catch it.'

'And how does your father travel to work?'

'He has his own coach that brings him from Hackney, down Cambridge Road. I used to make that journey with him every day before I married Matthew.'

'Could your father's coachman be prevailed upon to pick you and Doris up on the way?'

'I suppose so. Either that or make a separate journey after he's dropped Father off. It's only a mile or so down the road from here.'

'Very well,' Jennings announced. 'I have to see your father anyway, in order to arrange for Captain Curran to be placed in isolation, so I'll explain to him that Doris here has to be afforded the luxury of coach travel to and from her work, along with you, of course.'

'Oh la!' Doris said. 'I'll feel like Lady Muck, travelling in such style.'

'At least you'll remain alive,' Jennings muttered. 'And now it's time that I was going home.'

11

Those crushed into the overcrowded bus making its way westwards along Fleet Street began to suspect that they were travelling with someone slightly deranged as they listened to Jennings's increasingly wild imprecations when he read the headlines on the passing newspaper stands and listened to those hawkers' cries that were audible above the trundling rattle of his bus and the other wheeled conveyances that were sharing the busy rush hour street with it.

The best of them read '*Third nurse murdered — is "The Ripper" back among us?*', while others shrilled the more obvious '*Ripper strikes again — police helpless*', and '*Jack's back — come on, Police Commissioner!*'

Jennings did his best to creep along the corridor on his way to his office inside Scotland Yard, only to find Assistant Commissioner Atkinson already squeezed into the narrow space between the office desk and the wall.

'Well, Jennings? What have you to say for yourself? I take it you've read the morning papers?'

'Didn't need to, sir. The newsvendor headlines relieved me of that unpleasantness.'

'But they have a very good point, do they not? Why haven't you brought me the man who's doing this?'

'I will, once I catch him,' Jennings muttered. 'But at least I think I know who he is now.'

'Then why isn't he buckled and in a cell?'

'Because he's gone to ground somewhere in that cesspit called "the Irish community", that's why.'

'So who is he? Give me something I can use to get the Home Secretary out of my ear. Apparently Her Majesty interrupted her exhausting mourning regime for long enough to cable from her place of safety inside Osborne House, offering to make a rare appearance among her loyal subjects in London if it would assist.'

'At least it would make the streets more crowded and therefore safer from lone assassins, although I doubt that the royal carriage wheels would make it through the horse shit in Commercial Road. Anyway, in answer to your question, the man's name is "Logan" and until very recently he was a Captain in the Coldstream Guards. He was actually one of the victims of the Tower bombing, which I suspect that he was behind in the first place, and the victims of his murders — carried out, I believe, with his Army bayonet — were all nurses from the same ward in the London Hospital in which he was treated before his release.'

'So why murder nurses, if he's a Fenian?'

'Because they knew something of his connection with the bombing, sir. Something revealed by a patient in the bed next to his. It's all a little complicated to explain in a few minutes.'

'You've got all morning, as far as I'm concerned, Jennings, because I don't intend to move from here until you tell me what plans you have to buckle this lunatic. If you're right, then you'll be doing the Irish Branch's job for them at the same time, which will obviously be a feather in your cap and will prevent the Home Secretary using my balls for his next tennis game with the P.M.'

'As I already explained, sir, I need to hunt for this man inside the Irish community, and if I could perhaps borrow a couple of men who're more familiar with the Fenian Barracks, I have an urgent assignment for them in a low Irish drinking den in Wapping where I think my quarry may be skulking.'

'Undercover men, you mean?'

'Naturally. And they'd need to be good at their jobs. One whiff that we're after Logan and he'll be off into the far distance. He's also good at disguises, from what I can deduce.'

'I'll see what I can do,' Atkinson promised as he eased his bulk from behind Jennings's desk. 'In the meantime, let me have a full report on what you've discovered so far, so that I can at least pretend that we're on top of all this.'

Two hours later, the light from the hallway was blocked out by human bulk. Jennings looked up sharply from the report he was just completing and saw two men who looked for all the world like coal haulers from the London Docks.

'Lonergan and Doyle, Inspector,' the taller of them announced.

Jennings waved them into his office and apologised for the fact that he had only one visitor's chair. 'I assume that "Lonergan and Doyle" are not a firm of solicitors?'

'Never heard that one before, sir. We're from the Irish Branch. Michael Lonergan and Patrick Doyle.'

'With names like that, you sound as if you just got off the ferry in Liverpool,' Jennings observed, 'and which of you is which?'

'I'm Lonergan, sir,' replied the man who thus far had done all the talking. 'And our names are real, since our grandfathers did indeed come off the ferry at some time in the past. But you have to admit that names like that make it much easier for us to blend in with the clientele in any Fenian hangout, to be sure, to be sure.'

'You don't sound very Irish — or at least, you didn't until you employed that hackneyed expression.'

'Don't need to sound Irish in here,' Doyle observed as he pushed himself off the wall on which he'd been leaning, 'and it's bad enough that we have to use that barbaric tongue when we're working out there.'

'I take it that "there" is The Harp, in Poplar?'

'That's it, sir. A very welcoming place if you're Irish. Absolutely deadly if you're not. We sit around the place subsidising the takings and looking and sounding as if we just came off the boat and are in search of gainful employment. The profits all go to a gombeen called "Brennan", although the licensee calls himself "O'Connor".'

'And what "gainful employment" have you been offered so far?' Jennings asked suspiciously. 'Nothing unlawful, I hope?'

'Just a bit of extra muscle at meetings, of which there are many in that neighbourhood,' Lonergan told him with a sly warning look towards Doyle. 'And no, we haven't yet learned who was behind that Tower bomb, else we'd be back on surveillance duties in Liverpool.'

'Well, I have something "gainful" for the pair of you,' Jennings told them. 'I want you to go to The Shamrock in Wapping. Ever heard of it?'

'Better than that, we've visited it, as ambassadors of The Harp,' Doyle explained with a grin. 'I'm rather handy with the darts, so whenever the challenge goes out from one Irish pub to another, I'm the first choice from The Harp. And Michael here comes along as my bodyguard, since these matches can sometimes finish up with the rival team as the target.'

'Your new commission is to go back to The Shamrock and find someone called Logan — Gerard Logan. A suspected Fenian sympathiser.'

'Why do you want him found, and what do you want done with him when we do?' Lonergan asked.

Jennings explained all about Logan's suspected involvement in both the Tower bombing and the murder of three nurses. 'So if you locate him, keep him under observation and get word back to me immediately, understood? No playing the hero and leaving the man half dead so that he can't be interrogated as soon as he's brought in.'

'What does he look like?' Doyle asked.

Jennings shrugged. 'All I can tell you is that he's tall. If it helps, he used to be a Coldstream Guards Captain until he went to ground, and he left the London Hospital sporting his former uniform.'

'That should make him easier to find,' Lonergan said. 'Although if he's wearing that inside an Irish pub, our first sight of him may be as a corpse.'

'Obviously he won't be,' Jennings frowned. 'But he'll still have access to it, and the Fenians may have a use for such a disguise. I believe that Logan's currently in possession of a long dark cloak of some sort and a wide-brimmed hat. He'll also still be showing signs of recent burns to the face.'

'To which we can add burns to the arse,' Doyle said. 'You want us to start today? And do we get our beer money from your department now, instead of our own?'

'Why have I been moved into this single room?' Tom Curran demanded of Matthew as he slipped into the isolation ward. 'I was supposed to be going home in a few days. Has something happened? Have I become infectious?'

'There's absolutely nothing to worry about — you have my word on that as a man of God,' Matthew assured him, 'and we've arranged for Rose to visit you today, in order to bring

130

you the clothes you'll need when you leave here in two or three days' time.'

'Then who's he?' Curran demanded as he nodded towards Jennings. 'Another doctor? A fever specialist or something?'

'You really *don't* have any need to concern yourself over your health,' Matthew assured him. 'Surely you know me well enough by now to trust me not to lie to you?'

'You've certainly been very kind, to me *and* Rose,' Curran confirmed. 'I'm sorry if I seem a little ungrateful, and perhaps I'm letting my nerves run away with me. I've never been quite at ease in my mind since that dreadful explosion.'

'How much do you remember of it?' Matthew asked, seizing the opportunity.

Curran shook his head. 'Nothing after when we took our seats at the dinner table. There's a huge gap after that, until when I woke up in this hospital, screaming with pain. I remember a doctor telling a nurse to give me something for the pain, then the next thing I knew I was lying in a bed in that ward and a lovely nurse was cooling my forehead and asking me if I needed something more for the pain. I drifted in and out of consciousness for days and it was quite a shock when Rose turned up and told me I'd been lying there for a week.'

Matthew judged the time to be right as he turned and indicated Jennings. 'This is a friend of mine, John Jennings. He works at Scotland Yard, and he's been asked to go in search of whoever it was that planted that bomb.'

'Fenians, they reckon,' Curran replied, then looked up at Jennings. 'Have you found out how they managed to smuggle it into the Officers' Mess?'

'I was hoping that you could help me with that,' Jennings replied with the most encouraging smile of which he was capable. 'But you say you can't remember anything after you took your seats at the banquet table? Not even who was sitting where?'

'I can just about picture that in my mind,' Curran agreed, 'but everything after that's just a blank.'

'Well, let's start with that, shall we?' Jennings invited him. 'Who was on your immediate left, for example?'

'That was John Sweeney. He got off lucky, with only chest wounds. He was discharged last week some time. Can't remember precisely when — it's all a bit fuzzy.'

'And to the right of you, closer to the Lieutenant-Colonel?' Jennings persevered.

Curran's brow furrowed as he did his best to recall the scene. 'Jeremy Mullens, to the best of my recollection. They tell me he's dead.'

'That's right, he is, I'm afraid,' Jennings confirmed, 'along with the Lieutenant-Colonel and the man on his other side — remember who that was?'

'George Kelly, I think. And beyond him Jim Owen, then Peter Hargraves. They're still on that ward that I was on — surely you could ask them what they remember?'

'I already did, but they seemed to be experiencing the same memory blackout as you,' Jennings lied. 'But what about the man on the far right-hand end of the table — Gerard Logan?'

Curran looked thoughtful for a moment, then shook his head. 'Was he there as well? He must have been, I suppose, since he organised everything that day and it would be out of character for that slimy toad to miss a free feed.'

'You don't remember him being in the bed next to you on the ward?' Matthew asked gently.

Curran looked back in surprise. 'Was that Logan? The man with his face covered in bandages? That makes sense, I suppose, since he seemed to spend all his time moaning and complaining, although the voice didn't sound like his. Still, what with the morphine and everything…'

'And that was Gerard Logan's normal manner, was it?' Jennings asked.

Curran nodded. 'A thoroughly unpleasant piece of work. Morally defective and very unpleasant company. He was in danger of being thrown out, I think, because of his gambling, and as for his wife — well, the less said the better.'

'Let's be clear about this,' Jennings persisted, 'you had no idea that the man in the next bed to yours was Gerard Logan?'

'None whatsoever — mind you, his face was covered in bandages and most of the time I was drifting in and out on that morphine stuff, thank God.'

'But you seemed to take exception to him, according to the nurses,' Matthew told him.

Jennings gave Matthew a warning tap on the shoulder, then quickly enquired, 'What *was* it about Gerard Logan that you disapproved of, exactly?'

'Just the whole manner and demeanour of the man. I wasn't the only one who considered it a mistake that he'd been commissioned in the first place, since he didn't have the necessary moral fibre for officer status. His gambling, his fondness for other women, the dreadful company he kept on his days off and the way he seemed to turn a blind eye to his wife prostituting herself. A dreadful person altogether. And … and … something else, but I can't quite put my finger on it.'

His face had hardened as he completed his assessment of Logan, and Jennings opted to push the point. 'Something about the day of the explosion?'

'Yes. No. I mean, I don't think … that is, *perhaps*, but I can't quite get it into focus. I'm sorry. I guess I'm just as useless in my mind as I am in body, thanks to whoever planted that bomb.' He became agitated and looked wildly from Matthew to Jennings, then back again. 'Am I losing my mind?'

'I'm sure it's just the stress of attempting to relive that dreadful moment that turned your life around,' Matthew assured him gently as he placed a hand on his forehead. 'Just pray to God for the light to be cast upon the road that you must walk and He will not forsake you.'

'Even if your memory has,' Jennings replied coldly as he gestured with his hand for Matthew to leave with him.

'That was a bit harsh,' Matthew complained as they walked back down the hallway towards the staircase.

Jennings grunted. 'He's useless to me unless he can remember more than he has so far. Perhaps your father-in-law can inject him with a memory drug or something. I'll go and ask him, while you no doubt will be looking in on your wife.'

'I'll be ministering to the remaining patients, certainly,' Matthew replied, his voice heavy with disapproval. 'Someone has to give them reassurance, rather than treat them as mere sources of information.'

'I take it that the new travel arrangements are working successfully?'

'Indeed they are,' Matthew confirmed, 'and I think Doris has quite overcome her fear of being the next victim, given the comparative luxury of travelling to work and back in a coach.'

'She'll have to come back to earth when we catch the killer,' Jennings reminded him.

Matthew looked him firmly in the eyes as he replied, 'I think you mean *if*, don't you? It doesn't look as if poor old Tom Curran's going to be of any assistance in the matter of the Tower bomb, and you seem convinced in your own mind that cracking that case will also lead you to whoever's been attacking nurses.'

'It's a pity that God's blessings don't include the ability to join up leads,' Jennings said. 'Has the point not yet established itself inside your brain that whoever planted that bomb may be the same person who's been killing nurses? Look, I'll make it easy for you — who told Curran to keep his mouth shut, then took such an uncharacteristic interest in the identity of the nurses who'd overheard what Curran had to tell them?'

'You mean Logan?'

'Praise the Lord — the man's finally thinking logically and in straight lines!'

'But Curran obviously can't be of any help to you in respect of either of those matters.'

'We'll see about that. Off you go and play the dutiful husband and the bountiful man of God, while I go and bother Carlyle. I'm in need of a cuppa anyway.'

Carlyle looked up from the work he was doing with something immersed in formalin in a small tank and caught the look on Jennings's face. 'Put the water on to boil, Martin — by the look on the inspector's face he's already had a bad morning, which is to be regretted, since it's not yet eleven.'

'I'm here for more than tea,' Jennings said. 'I actually have need of your medical assistance.'

'An indiscretion with a lady of the night?' Carlyle asked.

Jennings waved his hand in irritation. 'Chance would be a fine thing, and I'm not here for one of your magic potions. I need to know if it's possible for someone to totally forget some dreadful event in his life, or if I'm being lied to by someone who's very convincing.'

'To what event are you referring?'

'The Tower explosion, of course.'

'And is the person with the blank memory one of the victims?'

'How did you guess? Captain Curran, as it happens.'

'And he claims to have no memory of the actual explosion, simply some trivial event that occurred slightly ahead of it in time?'

'Right on the money — you've come across this before?'

'Not personally, since I'm not a mentalist, but I've certainly read about it.'

'And what have you learned?'

'It's called "amnesia", which means, in layman's terms, "loss of memory".'

'I've heard of that, obviously,' Jennings replied, slightly offended. 'My grandfather reached the stage at which he didn't know who my granny was, because he'd forgotten that she ever existed.'

'That's not strictly speaking the same thing, Inspector, but it'll do for the time being. What I'm referring to is a very specific form of amnesia known as a "fugue". That's what you'd call a "mental blank".'

'And it's brought on by some dreadful experience?'

'Precisely. The human psyche is a delicate instrument, and it has therefore developed mechanisms and strategies to defend itself. If something happens which is too horrible to remember, the brain instructs itself to blot it out. To "dissociate" itself from it, if you prefer. That's why this form of memory loss has been labelled "dissociative amnesia".'

'So this bloke Curran can't remember anything about the explosion because his mind can't handle it, is that the picture?'

'A little judgmental, but basically correct. It's not his fault, you understand — he's not willing it to happen. He's just human, and try to imagine the sort of turmoil raging inside your head if you'd been through what he has and woken up minus an arm or a leg.'

'So there's no way to retrieve that lost memory?'

'Short of hypnotism, no. And that's not my department. Even if it were, there might be an ethical objection to employing it as part of a police enquiry.'

'Even an enquiry into a treasonous explosion that killed three Guards officers outright and wounded eight more — two of them fatally — in addition to the brutal slaying of three nurses?'

'You think that these matters are linked?'

'I'm convinced of it.'

'Even so, there might be ethical objections.'

'Not if nobody knew it had occurred.'

'I'll pretend I didn't hear that.'

Jennings uttered a soft curse and sat down heavily on a seat at the bench. 'A pity I wasn't with the nurse who was giving him morphine when he came out with what he now seems to have forgotten.' Then he looked back at Carlyle as he caught the strange expression on the doctor's face. 'What did I just say?' he asked.

Carlyle smiled. 'I'm not entirely sure, but I think you were telling me that this man Curran remembered what had happened while he was under morphine. Was that the case?'

'According to Nurse Mooney — the one who your coachman drives to work every day along with your daughter — that's what happened. Is that possible?'

Carlyle nodded. 'Not only possible, but quite a regular occurrence. One of the few light spots in a nurse's life is to listen to a patient's ramblings when they're under the influence of morphine. So far as anyone has ever been able to ascertain, those ramblings are an accurate reflection of what's on a patient's mind, and they sometimes contain references to their feelings of attraction to the nurse at their bedside, or they repeat in graphic detail some recent sexual encounter. They also often reveal things about the state of their marriage, so all in all a cheap, if somewhat sordid, form of entertainment.'

'Until the patient comes round and gets all embarrassed and swears them to secrecy, I suppose?'

'That's the beauty of it, Inspector — the patient has no recollection of what they've said, or for that matter any realisation that they've said anything.'

'So whatever this man Curran said to Nurse Mooney about Logan was probably accurate, and he'd have no memory of having said it?'

'Precisely. Not even any conscious memory of what his subconscious had revealed.'

'A pity that Nurse Mooney didn't take any detailed notes at the time. But whatever it was, it was enough to make Logan angry.'

'Wouldn't you be angry if someone said derogatory things about you? From what I can gather from the little that Adelaide has told me about matters on the Tower Ward, the two were hardly bosom companions.'

'But supposing that what Curran was saying had to do with the explosion?'

'Why would that annoy Logan, except to remind him of why he was lying in a hospital, uncertain of whether or not he'd spend the rest of his life with a white cane?'

'I haven't been keeping you up to date, but I've reached the stage in my enquiries at which I believe Logan to have been in some way complicit in that explosion and to have gone in search of nurses who, in his mind, could point the finger at him. Then he killed them.'

Carlyle reflected for a moment, then nodded. 'I always believed that there was something unusual in the fact that Logan had only facial burns and no other injuries. If he'd dived under the table, or even away from it at ground level, just as the bomb was detonating, then he'd have got the full force of the blast in the form of a flash of searing flame, but no flying objects that would sever limbs, or pepper him with shards of glass and wood.'

'So even the injuries that Logan sustained support my theory about him?'

'So far as concerns the explosion, certainly. As for the rest, it's obviously feasible, but there's nothing that Captain Curran can say that will support the rest of your conjecture that Logan then went on to commit those horrible murders.'

'There's nothing he can tell me even to support the explosion theory,' Jennings grumbled as he accepted the mug of tea and bit angrily into a shortbread biscuit. Then he caught the smile on Carlyle's face. 'There's no need to gloat,' he muttered.

Carlyle shook his head. 'I'm not gloating. I'm just wondering if we might get Captain Curran to oblige us with a replay of what he saw just before the explosion, or whatever he saw that might implicate Logan.'

'You told me earlier that it would be unethical.'

'What I actually said was that it would be unethical for me, a physician, to engage in a practice that is the province of a mentalist. However, the administration of morphine is well within my sphere of medical practice.'

'He's presumably no longer in need of pain relief?'

'How do you know? If it comes to that, how do *I* know? I've never had a limb amputated, thank God, but I've heard reports from other surgeons to the effect that unpleasant sensations related to the missing limb never go away.'

'So you'd be prepared to give him more morphine and hope that he comes out with something about the explosion?'

'Under closely controlled conditions, yes. He'll need to have a nurse with him and perhaps my God-fearing son-in-law, to create the comforting ambience of God's merciful blessings, or whatever else he chooses to call it. I'll obviously administer the morphine, to preserve the nurse's professional position, and we then note down what he says.'

'How can we be certain that his fevered brain will drift back to the explosion?'

'We can't, but it's our only option, so far as I can see. Unless you want to bring in a mentalist, that is, but that would involve a delay and some delicate negotiations in Harley Street.'

'When can we set about this?' Jennings asked eagerly. 'The sooner the better, so that I can buckle the lunatic.'

'I believe that Curran is due for discharge in a few days,' Carlyle replied, 'so I'll pretend that he's getting one more round of morphine to fortify his system prior to that happy moment. Arrange for the same nurse to attend him as on the previous occasion and bring along Matthew West to give the procedure some vestige of godliness. Let's say this time tomorrow, shall we?'

12

The group gathered around Curran's bed at the agreed hour and Carlyle inserted the ampoule, then withdrew after instructing Doris Mooney to sit with the patient while Matthew sat on Curran's other side, ready to note down everything he said. There had been something of an argument when Carlyle had suggested that Jennings's presence in the room might create a negative thought process in the patient, and he'd grown even more resentful when Carlyle had suggested Matthew as the witness who would record all that was said. Then Jennings had grudgingly withdrawn his objections when Carlyle had insisted that they either did things his way, or not at all.

Curran slipped into what looked like a deep stupor within seconds of the morphine entering his system, and his breathing became deep, regular and relaxed. Matthew was considering putting his notebook back in his jacket pocket when the breathing pattern altered, becoming more shallow and seemingly laboured. Matthew looked urgently across at Doris, who smiled reassuringly and told him, 'It's nothing to worry about — I think he's about to perform.'

Sure enough, the words began to come, hesitatingly and somewhat inarticulate to begin with, but within a minute what Curran was saying was distinct enough to allow Matthew to scribble it down hurriedly, fearful of missing a single word.

'Should have stopped him — checking the place settings my arse — traitor, that's what Logan is. He was only after his own ends. Looked uneasy even when we sat down. Sweating like the pig he is — always keeps looking under the table — should have asked him what he was about, but too late. The old man's on his feet — getting to the point at last — lifting the memorial plaque — bastard Logan's back under the table — Ah! *CHRIST*!'

The screams were stifled the minute that Doris leaned forward urgently and bathed Curran's head with cold water. Matthew breathed more easily and subconsciously adjusted his breaths to the deep rhythmic ones of the patient, as Doris looked anxiously across at him.

'Did you manage to get all that?' she whispered hoarsely. 'If not, I think I can remember most of it. It *was* him, wasn't it? Logan, I mean?'

'It certainly seems like it,' Matthew confirmed. 'Will you be alright to stay here with the patient while I pop outside and speak to Inspector Jennings?'

'Of course,' she assured him. 'He'll sleep for a few hours now, that's all. And Doctor Carlyle promised to look in on him after he's completed his morning rounds.'

Matthew made his way into the corridor, where he was all but attacked by an eager Inspector Jennings. 'Well?' he demanded.

Matthew smiled. 'You were right. You can arrest Logan for the Tower explosion whenever you can find him.'

Jennings lost no time in returning to the Yard and sending a cable to every police station in the East End, as well as a more detailed report to the Irish Branch, that Logan was to be located without delay and locked securely into the nearest police cell pending the arrival of the man who could confront him with his guilt of the Tower bombing. Then he went home and celebrated by taking his wife out for a roast beef supper at his favourite hostelry.

This euphoric mood lasted until the middle of the following morning, when the shadow darkening his doorway proved to be Michael Lonergan.

'Have you found Logan?' Jennings asked eagerly.

Lonergan shrugged. 'In a manner of speaking. Do you want the good news or the bad news?'

'The good news is that you've located Logan?'

'Indeed we have, but the bad news is that he'll be even more resistant to questioning that he might otherwise have been.'

'Meaning?'

'Meaning that he's dead. Fished out of the Thames early this morning, attired in his full dress uniform.'

Inspector Jennings stepped gingerly down Wapping Old Stairs, taking care not to lose his footing on the slippery vegetation that littered it following the recent high tide, and crunched his way along the gravelly beach that lay exposed as the tide retreated. A few hundred yards further east, he could see a group of uniformed police officers grouped around a prone form and he puffed his way towards them. One of them looked up and said something to the sergeant who appeared to be in charge, and it was to him that Jennings flashed his police badge.

'I gather that you have a stiff of considerable interest to me. It was left by the high tide, I take it?'

'Correct, Inspector,' the sergeant confirmed.

Jennings peered over his shoulder at the soggy bundle dressed in a military uniform. Not bothering to venture any further, he asked, 'How come you managed to identify him as Captain Logan?'

'Well, sir, as you can no doubt see for yourself, the uniform's that of a Coldstream Guards officer — you can tell that from the flashes. I happen to know that they're currently on Tower duty, on account of that explosion a few weeks back, so I sent a messenger up there as soon as we found the corpse. There's a sort of serial number on the inside of the jacket collar, and the Tower confirmed who the uniform had been issued to. Then I remembered the cable we all got from you, asking us to be on the lookout for a man called "Logan" who'd gone absent without leave from the Coldstreamers, and it was me that alerted your man Lonergan. Are you from the Irish Branch, and is it true that the bloke lying there was the one who did that bombing?'

'No and yes, Sergeant, but we don't have time for that. Any idea how long he's been in the water?'

'Probably only last night, sir. He's still kind of fresh by the standards of the stiffs we pull out of here, and the night shift at the fixed post down in Shadwell had a complaint of rowdy behaviour along the waterfront around midnight. Seems that a couple of drunks were carrying on, singing and what-not, one of them carrying the other on his shoulder, like he was legless. One of them was reported as being a soldier, and we put two and two together. If the man went into the water down in Shadwell, the incoming tide would have washed him this way and then left him high and dry where you can see him on the shingle.'

'Excellent work, Sergeant,' Jennings beamed, 'and I'll see that it's reported in the appropriate quarter. Your shoulder flash tells me you're based in Whitechapel, and I know Chief Inspector Shanahan very well.'

'Yes, sir, thank you, sir. What do you want done with the corpse?'

'On a handcart up to the London Hospital mortuary, for the attention of a Doctor Carlyle.'

Two hours later, the air began to come out of Jennings' inflated expectations. Down in the mortuary, Carlyle was waiting with a long face, a naked body stretched out on the table in front of him and a pile of sodden army uniform garments on the floor by his side.

'I hope you haven't called off the search for Logan,' he announced glumly as Jennings's gleaming smile appeared in the doorway.

'Not yet, but I'll get round to it. I just called in to get the death certificate for the man you've obviously been carving up.'

'You can have that, certainly, once you give me a name,' Carlyle replied.

Jennings's brow furrowed in annoyance. 'Didn't they tell you it was Logan?'

'They did, but it isn't.'

'Come again?'

'The man lying on this slab was not your man Logan,' Carlyle insisted.

'But the uniform was identified at the Tower as having been issued to Logan,' Jennings protested as his spirits began to sag.

'The uniform may well have been the one issued to Logan,' Carlyle insisted, 'but the man inside it wasn't him.'

'How can you be certain?' Jennings challenged him.

Carlyle smiled weakly. 'Because I'm a pathologist who was trained to look beyond the end of his nose, and I briefly met Logan when I treated him in Casualty Reception on the night of the Tower bombing.'

'But his face would have been horribly burned, so how can you be certain?'

'Precisely for that reason. This man has no sign of any burn marks to the face, recent or otherwise. This alerted my suspicions, so I examined the uniform more carefully. Army tailors are among the best in the country and would never have allowed an officer to walk abroad in Dress trousers that were at least an inch too short, or a jacket whose sleeves ended halfway down the thumb.'

Jennings hurled his hat at the wall and sat down heavily on the chair by the door reserved for visitors.

'If it makes you feel any better,' Carlyle told him, 'I can confirm that this man drowned. Most likely because he was unconscious when he entered the water. The large lump on the back of his head made that more likely. Does that accord with your other information?'

'Only too fully,' Jennings said. 'There was a report of one man carrying another in what looked like a homeward journey by two drunks, one of them dressed as a soldier. I'll take a guess that the military type was your man on the slab and that the one carrying him was Logan, anxious to throw us off the scent by faking his own death. He must have whacked his victim over the noggin earlier in the journey, but that now raises two questions. The first is the identity of the man in the uniform, and you can probably guess the second.'

'The current whereabouts of Logan?'

'Precisely. Time I made use of the extra manpower I've been allocated.'

Lonergan and Doyle looked apprehensive as they answered the summons to Jennings's office and learned of the discovery of the man badly disguised as Logan, interspersed with every oath they had ever heard and several that they were able to add to their repertoires.

'So what have you two lazy buggers got to report to me, other than how much beer you've knocked back at public expense?' Jennings demanded, white in the face with suppressed rage.

Lonergan held out a peace offering. 'Your dead man was calling himself "Corcoran", although that probably wasn't his real identity. They all seem to go under false names down in The Shamrock.'

'How did he come to have the uniform?' Jennings demanded.

Doyle opted to demonstrate that he could also convey recent intelligence. 'Seems he either bought it, or perhaps borrowed it, from a man called "Lachann". Something of a hero in The Shamrock, but only by name.'

'So you've never actually seen him?'

'Not so far as we're aware,' Lonergan admitted. 'It's all very "hush-hush" and "needs to know" in that place. Except for the rumour that the uniform was to be used in a raid on the Tower Armoury. They were looking for volunteers.'

'I hope you didn't?' Jennings asked sharply.

Lonergan sighed. 'We intended to advise you of this planned raid as soon as we could get more information on who was taking part in it, and it occurred to us that we might need your approval to put our hands up for it, in order to get you those names.'

'Permission denied!' Jennings snapped. 'Have you, during your wild carousing, come across anyone answering Logan's description?'

'Not physically, no,' Doyle replied, 'but I'm beginning to think that your man "Logan" is in fact the man they're calling "Lachann", given the similarity in the name and the fact that he seems to have been in a position to supply a military uniform.'

'I think I could have worked that out for myself without the assistance of a gallon of stout,' Jennings all but snarled. 'You haven't, I take it, actually *seen* this "Lachann" character?'

'No, like Michael already said, it's all very secretive and under the table, if you get my meaning,' Doyle replied. 'The top men seem to control things from a distance and it's only the pit ponies you see in the bar, awaiting instructions from the heroes.'

'Well, find him — and *fast!*' Jennings ordered them. 'Remember that his face will bear all the signs of having been in a recent bonfire, due to his stupidity in peering under the table just as the bomb went off in the Tower Barracks. It looks as if it might have been detonated when the Lieutenant Colonel lifted the memorial plaque off the dinner table, so keep your ears open also for anyone skilled in rigging bombs.'

'Explosives merchants with facial scarring,' Lonergan muttered sarcastically. 'That covers just about every regular patron of The Shamrock. Do we get a bonus for producing a dozen?'

'Get out while the going's good!' Jennings growled ominously, and the two Irish spies beat a hasty retreat.

'You're too late for supper, I'm afraid,' Adelaide told Jennings as she opened the front door and found him standing there in the pale light of an early August half-moon.

'After the dinner I had, that's probably all to the good,' Jennings managed to smile grimly. 'Is everyone home, and may I come in to report the latest news?'

'Of course. We're all in the sitting room, and I can at least offer you a cup of tea.'

Matthew and Doris looked up expectantly as Jennings entered the sitting room, but it was Doris who asked the question.

'Have you caught him yet?'

'No,' Jennings told them with a defeated air as he took the remaining armchair and smiled up at Adelaide gratefully as she handed him the teacup. He then recounted the day's events, together with a tactfully worded expression of his disappointment with the way things had worked out. 'So,' he concluded, 'Logan still eludes us and for the time being we have to assume that Doris is still a target. That means that she has to remain here for the foreseeable future and travel to and from the hospital in the coach.'

'That's no hardship for any of us,' Adelaide said kindly to Doris. 'If anything, it's a bonus having a trained nurse living with us while Florence is going through this dreadful teething stage.'

'And dear Florrie is *so* sweet!' Doris added, receiving a frown from Adelaide.

'Please don't use that name, even if my husband does,' she insisted. Adelaide transferred her gaze to Jennings. 'I take it that the night shift nurses are still being escorted backwards and forwards to the hospital by your uniformed officers, Inspector? To judge by their giggles and excited chatter when they come onto the ward for the shift change, they're thoroughly enjoying the attention and I think that Alice may be getting quite sweet on one of them.'

Jennings nodded. 'We've been assuming that Logan's targets were the nurses who were on that night duty when Curran shot his mouth off. Doris here is the sole survivor of that team, and we've taken all these precautions with her in the belief that Logan will be awaiting his chance. But in case we're wrong in that, we can't afford to expose the day shift nurses to the same risk, which is why they still have the police escort. From what I hear, no-one on either side is complaining about that, so we'll allow that arrangement to continue as well.'

'What about Captain Curran?' Matthew asked. 'I would have rated him as being at an even higher risk of attack than Doris.'

'You're probably right about that,' Jennings agreed, 'particularly since the poor bloke only has one arm to defend himself with. But we provided a heavy guard for the family's removal to their new home in Berkshire, and we still have a regular lookout detail on the only entrance to the farm that he's managing, on which the family are also living. So hopefully that narrows things down to Doris.'

'Thanks,' Doris muttered.

Adelaide leaned sideways on the sofa that they were both occupying in order to place a protective arm around her. 'No need to rub it in, Inspector,' she said, 'but let's maintain an optimistic outlook, shall we? Do you still have your spies in the Irish community?'

'I *do*, but their value at present is limited,' Jennings explained, 'since everyone within that Irish community is playing "hunt the thimble" in the low alehouse where we believe that Logan's being hidden away. He may be the man using the name "Lachann", and if so then he's highly regarded within the Fenian Brotherhood and no-one's likely to give him up.'

'You have men inside that place?' Matthew asked.

Jennings nodded. 'But don't hold your breath. They're Irish themselves, for one thing — or at least, their ancestors were. Added to which, they're being supplied with beer money to just sit in there and pass on what they hear. I suspect that the booze goes to their ears.'

'This is The Shamrock?' Matthew asked. 'The place I alerted you to?'

'Correct,' Jennings confirmed.

'And what you're hoping is that the men you've positioned in there will spot Logan, or whatever else he's calling himself?'

'Also correct.'

'Wouldn't they be better positioning themselves outside, watching for the man to come and go from there?'

'I'm sure they've thought of doing that, but of course that would make them more conspicuous,' Jennings reminded him. 'And they wouldn't be able to hear what was being said *inside* then, would they?'

'So what are you more interested in?' Matthew challenged him. 'Finding Logan, who at present is easily spotted because of his burn marks, but won't be once they've had time to heal? Or are you more intent on proving that you know better than the Irish Branch and can deliver a load of intelligence information that will no doubt see you one step further up the career ladder?'

'Matthew!' Adelaide remonstrated, just before Jennings himself rose to his feet angrily.

'I'll pretend I didn't hear that, but at least my focus is on someone we know exists — not that po-faced worker of miracles whose cause you're always championing. A pity he couldn't turn water into Guinness, then at least this wouldn't be costing so much to the public purse!'

'*Damn* the public purse!' Matthew said. 'We're talking about preserving the life of this lovely young lady who's devoted her life to the nursing of others, and all *you* seem capable of doing is moaning about the cost of it all and stuffing around inside a low alehouse when your men should be scouring the streets!'

'I'll see myself out,' Jennings replied huffily as he headed towards the living room door, leaving Adelaide red-faced and embarrassed.

'Are you still annoyed with me?' Matthew asked two hours later as they lay in bed, secure in the knowledge that if Florence woke up in the room next door Doris would be there to cuddle and reassure her, prior to coaxing her into swallowing some more of 'Mrs Winslow's Syrup'.

'Not annoyed, so much as frustrated and not a little embarrassed,' Adelaide replied starchily. 'The man's doing his best and has gone to a lot of trouble to keep Doris safe. Remember her — the "lovely young lady", as you called her?'

'Is *that* it?' Matthew chuckled. 'Are you jealous?'

'Don't be so ... so ... so *male*,' Adelaide muttered. 'Of course I'm not jealous, but I am concerned when my own husband goes out of his way to annoy the very man we're all relying on for Doris's continued life.'

'Well, the man doesn't know what he's about,' Matthew protested, earning a snort from Adelaide.

'And you do, of course, with your years of experience in police procedure?'

'My years of experience with working-class people, anyway,' Matthew replied. 'You forget that I spent several years out in the streets of the East End, preaching the Gospel to these people on market days. Just down the road from The Shamrock, as it happens, in Shadwell. If nothing else I got to watch them come and go, and if Logan gets within a hundred yards of me I reckon I could spot him.'

'You talk as if you were thinking of going back to street preaching.'

'I am — outside The Shamrock,' he replied quietly.

Adelaide sat bolt upright in bed to glare down at him in the half light. 'I forbid it!'

'You can't,' Matthew reminded her. 'We agreed before our marriage that each of us would be free to live our lives as we wished and that neither of us would seek to prevent the other following their life's desires.'

'That was before you became my husband and the father of a little girl who hasn't yet attained her first birthday. Follow your life's desires if you wish — and I've never once sought to persuade you away from preaching a lost cause — but what you're suggesting sounds more like a *death* wish. And what do you propose to do if you *do* spot Logan, even assuming you can identify him without his bandages, which are all you ever saw him with?'

'The scars will give him away. And if and when I spot him, I'll get word to Jennings, then follow him to wherever he's skulking.'

'Have you been at the communion wine again?'

'A cheap jibe. In any case, it's barely alcoholic.'

'But you're talking like a man who's had too many. Idle boasting, talking through your — well, talking nonsense anyway. It'll all seem different in the morning, you'll see.'

But when the early start came as usual and Doris had insisted on clearing the breakfast dishes ready for Mrs Dunning to wash them in the sink, Matthew walked out into the front hall where their coats were kept and returned wearing the heavy weatherproof cape that he had retained from his street-preaching days.

'Why are you wearing that cloak?' Adelaide asked suspiciously.

Matthew smiled down at her. 'The weather looks a little inclement for the time of year.'

'You're going street preaching, aren't you?' she demanded accusingly.

He nodded. 'I wasn't joking, you see — nor was I drunk.'

'Do you intend to alert Jennings to what you're proposing to do?'

'Why should I, only to hear him forbid it, because he wants all the glory from this? If you want him to know what I'm up to, *you* tell him.'

'Don't think I won't!' Adelaide fired back. 'But before you go, at least give me one last kiss to remember you by.'

The coach came on time and as soon as it arrived at the hospital, Adelaide hurried into the general office and asked to use the telephone.

13

Matthew drank in the memories as he took up his position in the middle of Tench Street, directly across the narrow thoroughfare from The Shamrock. Street preaching was no challenge to him, although it was now a year or two since this had been his regular way of life, as an eager young preacher attached to the Wesleyan Mission only a few streets away from where he was now holding his battered Bible high in the air and clearing his throat prior to proclaiming God's holy word to those passing by who'd be prepared to listen.

Then along had come Adelaide, he reminded himself, and as if her accepting his offer of marriage had not been one of God's miracles in itself, he had, while working alongside her and her father, had occasion to visit St Dunstan's Church in Stepney, investigating the murder of its then curate. One thing had led to another and the current vicar, Joseph Mulholland, had recognised in the fervent, honest and pure-hearted Matthew the perfect replacement for the dead curate and now here he was — married to the most beautiful and entrancing woman he had ever met, the father of the most delightful little daughter and privileged to be serving God in the oldest and wealthiest parish in the East End.

Yes, God was indeed the source of all his blessings, and the least he could do was to share with his fellow creatures the good news that God was always with them and that His mercy and undying love could turn around all their drab and seemingly purposeless lives. Inspired by that thought alone, he opened his heart at the same time as his mouth and began to preach, all the while keeping a lookout across the lane for a tall man with facial scars.

The initial responses were those to which he'd become accustomed during his self-appointed orations at the Saturday markets just a few hundred yards back along the High Street. It was only an ordinary midweek day today, but those who heard what he was confidently preaching into the warm air reacted in just the same way as they had done on market days.

Some stopped to take in his words and looked for a hat, a sack or a basket on the ground in front of him, as they would for a street performer begging for alms. Others appeared to ignore him completely as they slid, shamefaced, past him, in furtherance of their own ongoing sin. Another group might regard him as an object of amusement and earn the plaudits of their shabby associates by hurling witty obscenities in his direction. He bore all this patiently, reminding himself that those who had gone before him, particularly his great heroes John and Charles Wesley, had been the target of physical missiles as well as verbal ones, but had never once been deflected from their inspired mission.

Then there were those who opted to engage him in religious debate, not always in a friendly way, but he was hardened against those as well. So the large man who swayed through the door of The Shamrock across the road, then stopped when he heard Matthew preaching, seemed no different from the others he had engaged in lively discourse. He was clearly the worse for drink, to judge by his unsteady gait as he walked the few feet across the busy street, and Matthew sadly reminded himself that noon was still a good while away and that for those as deeply in the thrall of liquor as this man must be, God had an ever open hand to guide them along the road to sobriety.

'Do ye believe all that gobshite?' the man demanded aggressively.

Matthew gave him his best smile as he nodded. 'Indeed I do, sir, since God has filled my life with love and blessing.'

'He's filled yer head wi' shite, more like,' the man retorted as he spat on the ground at Matthew's feet. A few passers-by stopped out of curiosity, in the hope that a rude exchange of opposing prejudices might lead to an impromptu fist fight, and Matthew persevered, since any audience was better than none.

'Do you deny the redeeming beauty of Christ's love and God's overpowering strength over the forces of darkness?' Matthew asked.

The man gave a mocking laugh with an edge to it like a saw going through metal. 'Yer a brave eejit, I'll say that for ye,' he said, red in the face. 'Standing outside an Irish pub preaching all that Protestant blasphemy!'

'The word of God is never blasphemous,' Matthew insisted, earning himself another harsh laugh as the man loomed closer.

'It is when it comes from the scabby mouths of gombeens like you. It was your sort that claimed to have conquered Ireland, waving their prayer books in one hand and their sabres in the other. Poisoning our crops, violating our women and reducing our children to slavery. Was that the work of God, are ye trying to tell me?'

'I was never once in Ireland in my entire life,' Matthew insisted, 'so I cannot answer for those who were. But if they carried the word of God in their hearts, then their motives must have been pure.'

'Is that right? Then you and me certainly worships a different God. Their motives was to stamp on a proud nation, to reduce God's chosen people to the level o' beggars. An' they did that in the name o' God. The same God that's comin' out o' your mouth like a shower o' sick!'

The crowd had grown considerably, and the man clearly had a few supporters among them who were of the same persuasion, several of whom had drifted out of the pub across the road. Matthew was used to challenges like this, if not quite so fuelled by the demon drink, and he stood his ground.

'What's coming out of my mouth is God's pure truth, even if the Devil has so befuddled your wits with the liquor with which he beguiles so many that you can't hear it.'

'Pissed, is it?' the man screamed as he lunged towards Matthew with open bear-like arms. 'Well, whatever's comin' out o' your mouth won't be for much longer. Here's yer Heavenly reward!'

The man must have weighed as much as one of the horses that pulled the buses, Matthew estimated as he was all but flattened into the ground by the impact of the man's dive upon him. All the breath left his body as he was obliged to twist his head first one way and then another, to avoid the flurry of fists aimed at it. He was still jerking his head from side to side when the sun shining directly in his eyes told him that the man was no longer on top of him. He scrambled to his feet in time to see his assailant being held firmly at each arm by two burly men who were busily occupied in attempting to tie his wrists together. Still groggy from the attack, he turned at the sound of the familiar voice.

'You stupid, stubborn *idiot!* You just ruined a perfectly good police operation!'

Jennings had recovered his composure, if not his peace of mind, as he walked into the cell whose metal gates had been opened for him by the turnkey in charge of the common cells below ground in Whitechapel's Leman Street Police Station. At his back were two burly uniformed constables, just in case, and as the cell door clanged behind them all, the man in the corner rose to his feet.

'Is this when you an' yer English bullies gives me the clatters round the noggin? Bring it on, 'cos Sean Finnegan can take it!'

Jennings smiled unpleasantly as he signalled with his hand for the two constables to step back a pace. 'Thank you at least for revealing your name. That will make it much easier when we advise your cronies in The Shamrock that you've told us a pretty tale, since at least we can reveal the source of our information about their treasonous activities.'

Finnegan looked uncertain for the first time that morning. 'What are ye drivellin' on about?' he demanded, receiving another smirk from Jennings.

'You have a choice, Mr Finnegan. You are at present detained for attacking a man of God going about his lawful business. That is probably enough to earn you a seven-month stretch in Newgate, where you can no doubt celebrate your joint ancestry with others who chose to cross the Irish Sea in the belief that they could somehow overthrow Her Majesty's Government. But the quality — and indeed the length — of your days in a communal cell with fellow shit-stirrers may well owe a lot to what we tell them about your level of co-operation with the enemy.'

'Talk in English, yer gobshite!' Finnegan demanded.

Jennings duly obliged. 'Only you and I, and of course my two associates here, will know what it is you're about to tell us about the network of treason that exists inside The Shamrock and for that matter its sister establishment, The Harp in Poplar. If it is made known that you gave us names, addresses, details of further planned outrages and suchlike, then I doubt that your days alive inside an Irish-infested cell along the road in Newgate would need more than one hand to count.'

'I'll be tellin' ye nothing o' that nature!' Finnegan insisted, but the smile didn't leave Jennings's face.

'I have no doubt that such is your current intention and belief, Mr Finnegan. But as I already pointed out, only those of us here this morning will know that to be the truth. If those with whom you are subsequently locked away are told something different, then it would be only your word that you told us nothing, would it not?'

Finnegan's face lost most of its colour as the realisation set in. 'Ye wouldn't!'

'I would. Now — are we about to do business?'

'Meanin'?'

'Meaning that I require only a small amount of information from you, regarding just one man. If I receive it to my satisfaction, then you'll be held here until your trial, then consigned within the walls of Newgate for whatever period a magistrate deems appropriate, there to be reunited with your fellow countrymen.'

'And if I don't give yer that?'

'Then you'll be granted bail — in itself a sign that you ingratiated yourself with the authorities — and allowed back out onto the streets while certain of my other associates spread the word that you've sung like a canary regarding every foul and murderous deed that has been committed by the scum of Ireland for the past two years. I estimate that you'd make it as far as the London Dock gates before you became another victim of the unwritten code that has so successfully ensured that the Irish community in London is a law unto itself.'

'Who is it ye wish me to peach on?' Finnegan growled.

'I gather that he may now be calling himself Lachann, although I believe that his real name's Logan.'

'*That* chancer?' Finnegan replied as he spat onto the hard dusty floor. 'He's just a useless spanner wi' a high opinion of himself, an' that's the truth.'

'So you won't mind telling me where we could find him?' Jennings asked with a renewed smile.

Finnegan shook his head. 'Easier said than done. I've only ever seen him the once, when he was struttin' back like a rooster wi' a new set o' hens, showin' off his scars like they was diamonds.'

'His face still bears scars?'

'It did when I seen it — which was once too often, if yer seekin' a good opinion o' the man. If so, ask some other poor soul.'

'He keeps himself hidden, you say?'

'He does that. Mind you, wi' a face like that, so would I. But that doesn't mean he weren't once regarded as the great hero o' Erin, just because he let off a firework inside that Tower.'

'It's not denied that he was the one who caused the Tower explosion?'

'No, more's the pity. All we got ter hear about was how the stupid eejit stuck a banger under the table when they was all feedin' their faces, wired it to somethin' on the table, then sat there while it went off bang.'

'And he came back a hero, is that what you're saying?'

'Yeah, that was the way of it. He must be the first and only eejit to walk into the likes o' The Shamrock dressed as an English Army man and keep his wedding tackle intact.'

'He was wearing his Guards uniform?' Jennings asked by way of confirmation, in case he'd misunderstood the rich imagery.

Finnegan nodded. 'Not for long, though.'

'He gave it to someone else, didn't he?'

'Too bloody right an' he did. Conan Kelly — now there was a *real* hero o' Ireland.'

'Was?'

'That's right — was. He was all set to sneak into the Tower wearin' Logan's old uniform and kick down the doors to the Armoury inside o' there wi' the aid of a few more English weasels that's due a favour to the man that runs The Harp —'

'A man called Brennan?' Jennings asked eagerly.

Finnegan nodded at the same time as shooting Jennings a suspicious look. 'Yer well informed, it seems, so why does ye have to get any more from me?'

'Because you're preserving your miserable life by answering my questions,' Jennings reminded him. 'Why would men from inside the Tower be anxious to do favours for the man Brennan?'

'Fer the same reason as yer man Logan — they made the mistake o' playin' at the cards wi' Brennan, till they owed him so much money that not even handin' over their first born woulda repaid the debt.'

'So Logan agreed to plant the explosive in the Tower in order to repay a gambling debt?'

'Was I not just after sayin' that he did? Are ye listenin'?'

'Then why did he agree to hand his uniform over to Kelly?'

'Same reason. In addition ter which, he was in debt ter Kelly for more gambling losses. That was Kelly's big mistake, they reckons. Logan couldn't use the uniform clobber anymore anyway, on account of the fact that he woulda been on a fizzer had he showed his mug back in the Tower, so he comes the raw maggot by agreeing ter hand it over ter Kelly so that he could play the hero in the Armoury raid, then the two o' them heads out inter the night air and next thing yer know Kelly's bin fer a swim in the river. That's when Logan hit the chute, on account of everyone in The Shamrock's wantin' ter plant him alongside his old mother what died fifteen years ago.'

'Logan's in hiding from his own criminal associates, you mean?'

Finnegan's face hardened. 'If by that shite remark yer referring to my loyal and stout-hearted Irish comrades, then please accept my expression of displeasure. But ye're right — Logan's life's not worth the livin' of it if he shows his face back in The Shamrock, on account of his sending Kelly to the fairies and at the same time putting the mockers on a great scheme ter make the English look even more stupid than they really are.'

'You have no idea where Logan may be skulking now?' Jennings persevered.

'Nah, an' if I did I swear ter God I'd be the first ter swing fer the useless gobshite.'

A very battered and bruised Matthew let himself into Curate's House and called a greeting to Violet Dunning, who had just finished feeding Florence and was busy putting her back down in her cot for her afternoon sleep. She took one look at Matthew's face and tutted as she gestured for him to go into the kitchen. She reached for the soap and flannel that lay on the draining board, then ignored his mild protests and expressions of pain as she cleaned up his dirt-streaked face and looked more closely at his injuries.

'You've lost a little bark off your face, but it'll mend. Mind you, that's a rare couple of bruises around your eyes. What possessed a man of your calling to go brawling in the streets? What will Mrs West have to say?'

'I'd rather you didn't tell her,' Matthew replied. 'As for how it came to happen, it was one of the prices we pay for attempting to preach the Lord's word to the heathen masses.'

'Saint Matthew's Epistle to the East Endians?' Violet jested.

Matthew smiled. 'That was very good, Mrs Dunning, but now if you'll excuse me I need to lie down for an hour or two. If my wife and Miss Mooney aren't back by the time you have to leave, just pull the front door to on the latch, if you'd be so good.'

14

Matthew awoke from a fitful slumber, in which he'd dreamed of his Sunday morning congregation leaving their pews and advancing menacingly on him armed with hymn books, to the sound of Adelaide and Doris coming through the front door. He heard the subsequent sound of boots on the staircase, which then moved into the second bedroom where Florrie was sleeping. Matthew assumed that it was Doris resuming her nursing duties. He eased himself painfully off the bed on which he'd slept in his clothes and wandered downstairs to the living room, where above the back line of the sofa he could see the long red hair piled up high, in the fashion of the day, where its owner sat skimming through the evening paper.

He leaned down and kissed the top of the head as he announced, 'After the day I've had, I can't imagine a more welcome sight than your beautiful face.'

'Matthew!' came a sharp voice behind him and he turned to see Adelaide in the living room doorway, with a sleepy Florence in her arms. Doris leapt up from the sofa, bright red in the face, and Matthew began to splutter an apology to them both.

Adelaide peered at his face. 'By the look of you, you've encountered more than my wrath today. That may explain why Inspector Jennings could barely articulate when he appeared on the ward this afternoon. He's invited himself over later this evening.'

'So, supper for four?' Matthew asked as jocularly as he could manage.

Adelaide frowned her special frown. 'Seemingly not. I issued the invitation, but he replied — and I quote his exact words — "The mood I'm in right now, putting me in the same room as Matthew with access to sharp instruments would not be a good idea." What *have* you done to annoy him? You went street preaching, didn't you?'

'I've no doubt that Jennings took great delight in giving you all the gory details, but I was only doing what I thought was for the best, since Jennings himself has proved just how useless the authorities can be when they stick to convention.'

'And running your own little show got you beaten to a pulp by some ape from an Irish pub that no-one in their right mind would attempt to stand outside, preaching an alternative religion. You call that a sensible plan? If I hadn't alerted Jennings to what I thought you were intending to do, *despite* my strictures to the contrary, I'd now be a widow.'

'It's very easy to be wise after the event,' Matthew replied in his best ecclesiastical tone, 'but I meant well and I'm still alive.'

'Thanks to Jennings and his bullies,' Adelaide reminded him. 'And from what I could make out between his oaths and imprecations when he came onto the ward for long enough to disturb the patients and scandalise the nurses, you ruined a plan that he'd instigated which was designed to find Logan.'

Matthew looked across at Doris, who was silently picking at her cottage pie and looking uncomfortable. 'Was Jennings *so* angry, or is Adelaide exaggerating in order to make me feel worse?'

'He used words I'd never heard before,' Doris said, 'and I've got two older brothers.'

'No doubt he'll come bearing an apology for his bad language and bluster,' Matthew suggested, receiving a snort from Adelaide as he pushed her half-eaten meal away from her.

'The only one who should be apologising is you, although I won't be holding my breath. And when he gets here, I'll clear the sitting room of anything that can be lifted by hand and thrown at you.'

An hour later the two men were glowering at each other from opposite sides of the sitting room, like two prize fighters being prepared by their trainers and seconds to enter the ring. Tea had been served, but no-one appeared to be in the mood to drink it as Jennings coughed awkwardly and mumbled an apology to Adelaide and Doris for his poor choice of words during his visit to the ward earlier in the day.

'No need to apologise,' Adelaide replied stiffly.

'I don't suppose anyone wants to hear what I have to say?' Matthew offered.

'Not unless it's your declared intention to leave the country and go and preach to the heathens,' Jennings snapped back.

'Look,' Adelaide intervened before Matthew could reply, 'it will obviously get us nowhere if you two behave like drunks on pay night. I assume that the reason for your visit, Inspector, is to bring us up to date with where your enquiries stand at present and suggest what we might do to assist — apart from desisting from quixotic gestures, that is,' she added with a stern glare at Matthew, who decided that his best option was to remain silent.

'Much though it pains me to say so,' Jennings told them all through thinned lips, 'Matthew's stupid exploit was not entirely valueless. The man who put him on the ground turned out to be a Fenian loudmouth called Finnegan, and when I introduced him to the delights of a cell underneath Leman Street Police Station he gave me the latest available intelligence on Logan's whereabouts. We have it confirmed that it was indeed Logan who planted that bomb in the Tower. Seems that he was able to put it under the dinner table, connected to the memorial plaque in such a way that it went off when the Lieutenant-Colonel lifted it up, but Logan obviously couldn't resist looking under the table from time to time, then looked once too often just as it went off. That explains how he came to have facial burns but no other injuries, because he was too far down the table for the impact to reach him. That led to him being regarded as a returning hero by the Irish cretins who hang around The Shamrock, until he killed one of their own.'

'The man in the military uniform?' Adelaide asked.

Jennings nodded. 'The very same. His name was Kelly, and Logan volunteered to give him his old uniform in order for Kelly to pose as an officer of the Coldstreamers and gain access to the Tower Armoury. I gathered from Finnegan that there are some other members of the Coldstreamers inside the barracks who've been corrupted by the Brotherhood, and I've alerted their commanding officer to that fact. It seems that dreadful man Brennan who all but owns The Harp, and certainly controls everything that goes on in there, is either very lucky at cards, or has a sleight of hand that he might be better off employing as a stage magician. Whatever the case, he encourages men like Logan to lose so much money to him in gambling sessions that they're then prepared to engage in treasonous activities in order to pay off their debts.'

'So that's how Logan got involved in the first place?' Adelaide concluded.

Jennings nodded. 'But it seems that even that experience didn't teach him the lesson it should have done. He then became indebted to Kelly, so when the two of them headed off after a gambling session in which they'd both had too much to drink, Kelly trying out his new uniform, Logan took his opportunity to solve two problems at the same time. Kelly's death wiped off his gambling debt and also — or so Logan hoped — suggested to the entire world that Logan was dead.'

'How do we know that he isn't?' Adelaide asked.

Jennings looked surprised. 'Your father didn't tell you?'

'I haven't seen him for over a week,' Adelaide explained. 'Very remiss of me, but Father tends to live like a hermit since my marriage, and unless I make a point of inviting him over to see little Florence it never occurs to him to drop in. I think he's apprehensive of passing on to his granddaughter some awful disease that he may have picked up from one of his corpses.'

'Well, it was the corpse in the uniform that informed him that it was not being worn by Logan at the time, employing those almost supernatural powers of his,' Jennings explained. 'Then Finnegan confirmed that, but gave us the additional information that the Irish have put the word out for Logan to be done in because he killed a valued member of their little coven.'

'So Logan's now on the run from Scotland Yard *and* the Fenians,' Matthew pointed out.

Jennings gave Adelaide the benefit of a sideways smirk. 'He's really quick, that husband of yours,' he quipped, but before Matthew could rise to it Adelaide added her own observation.

'Surely Logan won't be any danger to us now? He'll be too busy leaving the country, or at least London, surely?'

Jennings nodded towards Doris. 'Are you prepared to take that risk, either of you?'

It fell silent until Matthew asked, 'Presumably you've put the word out for him to be apprehended, along with his description?'

Jennings gave him the sort of look he reserved for his seven-year-old nephew. 'What do *you* think? We've got his description out to every mainline railway station, every coach company, every sea port and every police station in the country. It's really a question of whether we get him before the Fenians do.'

'That's my point!' Adelaide repeated excitedly. 'He'll be too busy keeping out of sight to want to risk any attack on Doris.'

'And I can only repeat my question of whether or not you're both prepared to take that risk,' Jennings replied. 'Logan will be thinking that there's still a possibility that Doris can reveal his involvement in the Tower bombing. He doesn't know that we've learned that already and have enough evidence to hang him for it. In his panicked mind he won't want to add the Army authorities to the growing list of those who're eager to bring him to justice, and may well be planning to eliminate the remaining nurse on his list of targets.'

'What about Major Curran?' Matthew reminded him. 'Isn't he at greater risk from Logan?'

'He would be if Logan could get to him,' Jennings replied. 'We've got him well guarded out on his market garden in Berkshire, and it would require Logan to venture into a wide open space. In the bustling and confined streets of the East End Logan can hide quite effectively, but in the countryside he'd stand out like a horse in a duck pond.'

'So I still have to remain in hiding here?' Doris asked feebly. 'I haven't seen my family for weeks now, and I feel very embarrassed having to rely on the goodwill and kind generosity of Adelaide and Matthew.'

'It can't be avoided, I'm afraid,' Jennings insisted.

It fell silent again until Matthew voiced the thought that had occurred to Adelaide as well. 'Please don't take this the wrong way, Inspector, but what precisely are the prospects of Scotland Yard actually finding Logan, given the recent developments?'

'Well, thanks to you we can no longer rely on gaining any new intelligence regarding his whereabouts from within the Irish community,' Jennings muttered.

To everyone's surprise, Matthew smiled. 'But if he's on the run from them as well, you wouldn't have gained any, would you? In fact, you wouldn't have known that he was on the run from them at all had I not given you Finnegan to interrogate.'

'You thinking of putting in for a reward or something?' Jennings asked sourly.

'You've only really got one way of flushing him out, haven't you?' Adelaide asked as she locked eyes with Jennings. 'Was that the real reason for your visit here this evening?'

Jennings couldn't meet her stare, but dropped his own gaze to the floor and nodded.

'Would either of you geniuses care to share your deep insight into what is being proposed that we do next?' Matthew asked with annoyance.

Jennings and Adelaide locked stares again.

'You tell them,' Jennings urged her, but she shook her head.

'It'll be your operation, so *you* tell them.'

'Tell us *what?*' Matthew demanded.

'I have to give him the chance to kill me,' Doris announced quietly and all eyes turned to her. She blushed slightly at being the centre of attention and continued. 'I'm the one he's after, and for as long as I hide away here he won't show himself. But if I go back to my old routine of walking to and fro between the hospital and the lodging house, then he'll take his chance. I assume that Inspector Jennings wants me to do that, but only with plenty of his men in disguise waiting to pounce.'

The silence was palpable, broken eventually by Jennings. 'Would you be prepared to do that, Doris?'

Before she could answer, Adelaide leapt in. 'I'm sure she would, but I'm not prepared to let her.'

'That's very kind of you, Adelaide,' Doris said in a small voice, 'but I'm a big girl now, and I'm ready to avenge Mary, Edith and Lily.'

'You just alluded to why I can't let you risk your life like that,' Adelaide replied with a steely look in her eyes. 'Miss Nightingale entrusted the safety of her highly trained and dedicated nurses to me, and three of them are dead. I wasn't to know that would happen, but there's no way on God's earth that, knowing what I know now, I'd be prepared to allow a fourth one to walk into the lion's den.'

'You obviously remembered something of the scriptures you were taught before cynicism set in,' Matthew said quietly, 'but may I remind you of another one? "Am I my brother's keeper"?'

'Keep your pomposity for the pulpit,' Adelaide replied dismissively, 'but you did, albeit indirectly, give me an idea earlier this evening.'

'I did?'

'You did. You leaned over the back of this sofa and kissed Doris on the head.'

'I've already apologised to you both for that,' Matthew sulked.

'You thought she was me, didn't you?' Adelaide said. 'At least, I hope you did. But regardless of your motives, Doris and I are remarkably similar in appearance. Roughly the same height and build and both with red hair. Logan only got a brief glimpse of Doris when he was introduced to her on the ward, along with the other three. He'll have only a fleeting memory of what she looks like and — dressed in her uniform and with my head down under her cap — I could pass for her.'

'But you're the mother of a small girl,' Matthew reminded her, 'as well as being my wife.'

'Please don't even *think* of saying something along the lines of "I forbid it", after the way you ignored my plea not to go preaching outside that awful pub,' Adelaide defied him, her eyes flashing.

Jennings coughed politely. 'Far be it from me to come between husband and wife, but Adelaide's idea reflects a damned sight more common sense than yours did, Matthew.'

'You just want to get Logan before the Fenians do,' Matthew protested, the colour rising in his face. 'You don't care how you achieve that — how many innocent lives you put at risk — so long as you get Logan's scalp nailed to your office wall!'

The two men glared at each other so fiercely that Adelaide rose hastily from her seat on the sofa to form a physical barrier between them. 'Matthew's about to apologise for that unworthy remark — *aren't you*, Matthew?' The look in her eyes as she turned to look at him was one with which he was familiar and to which there could be no resistance.

'If you insist,' he mumbled, 'but my point remains. Why don't we just let the Fenians kill him?'

'Because,' Jennings explained as he measured every word carefully, with a heavy dose of cold disdain, 'the public need to know that he's dead. You won't have forgotten the words that the less reputable of the newspapers expended on the suggestion that Jack the Ripper was back to his old tricks. If the Fenians get to Logan first, they're hardly likely to write a letter to the editor of *The Times* admitting their grubby deed, are they? If, on the other hand, the man is buckled, tried and hanged, not only for the Tower bombing but also the murder of the three nurses, then the people of the East End will be able to heave a sigh of relief.'

'You can't argue with that, Matthew,' Adelaide said, 'much though I'm sure you'd like to.'

'Not with that, no,' Matthew conceded, 'but I *can* argue with the suggestion that my wife — the mother of my child — offer herself as an open target for a lunatic.'

Far from being impressed by his concern for her welfare, Adelaide uttered a disgusted noise. 'I had never expected to hear such pompous, antediluvian and thoroughly objectionable drivel from the mouth of a man I always believed to share my own more enlightened beliefs. I exist in my own right, Matthew West, not simply because of my status as Florence's mother and *your* wife!'

'That came out wrongly,' Matthew pleaded in his own defence. 'I mean that I love you desperately and Florence needs a mother. See? I even got her name right, such is my concern.'

Adelaide tried not to giggle, but failed. As usual, Matthew's naive — almost schoolboy — openness had won her over, and despite herself she sat back down and kissed him lovingly, then blushed and looked down at the carpet.

It was Doris's turn to break the silence. 'Would you have any objection if it were *me* who exposed herself to Logan?' she asked of Matthew, and without thinking he conceded that his objection was more to do with who was to take the risk.

'I don't resent that in any way,' she said kindly, 'but it does tend to suggest that you have nothing against the *idea* — simply who's going to be the one walking along Brick Lane.'

'We haven't heard what the inspector has in mind yet, have we?' Matthew pointed out, and all eyes turned to Jennings.

'You've obviously got the general idea,' Jennings began. 'The lady we'll call Doris for the sake of argument will walk to and from the lodging house and the London Hospital, as if she's been on holiday for a while and has just resumed her duties. Remember that Logan will have been staking the route out every day, wondering what's happened to her in the past few weeks, and we can only hope that he hasn't seen her inside the hospital and has worked out what's been going on. Anyway, to repeat, she walks along her normal route and I'll have men everywhere, posing as street hawkers, street sweepers, shopkeepers and whatever. The minute he goes for the bait, we pounce.'

'I'll be accused of sour grapes, I know,' Matthew observed, 'but two things strike me immediately. The first is that if I were Logan I'd be wondering why the girls on the other shift are still benefitting from a uniformed police escort, while Doris is being allowed to go backwards and forwards unprotected.'

'I'd already thought that one out,' Jennings said complacently. 'Since the other three died, there's only been Doris left to make the daily journey backwards and forwards, because the Nightingale Nurses on the day shift have been replaced by nurses from the regular hospital contingent. I calculate that Logan will decide that police manpower constraints are such that we can't spare uniformed officers just for one nurse, and I'm banking on him being so desperate that he'll take his chance anyway; either that or he's so arrogant that he thinks he's outfoxed us. Now, what was your second objection?'

'I don't believe,' Matthew insisted, 'that your men could get close enough to Doris to prevent at least the first stabbing. If you recall, Mary was pulled off the street and dispatched very quickly with one sharp thrust of a sword. With Edith he must have been able to do something very similar, because she was dead and dragged over to that disposal bin in a quick flash of time before anyone else could come down the stairs into the yard. One swift stab and they're gone, so unless your men are virtually at his elbow, whatever they do will be too late to save the life of the victim.'

'I think you've persuaded me against it after all,' Doris said faintly as she reached for her teacup with a trembling hand.

'But not me,' Adelaide confirmed even more defiantly.

'Don't you think you should listen to whatever reassurance Jennings can give us, before you volunteer to have your throat slit?' Matthew objected, then transferred his gaze to Jennings. 'Well?' he insisted.

Jennings looked down at the floor. 'I won't deny that there'll be a risk,' he muttered, 'but my men are trained to watch body movements very carefully. They can tell, for example, when a man's about to throw a punch at them and they know enough about concealed weapons to deduce that one's being carried simply by noting how a person's walking or standing. Logan would need to reach inside his cloak to produce his weapon, which I'm convinced is a bayonet, and in the time it'll take him to do that my men will have pounced.'

Matthew snorted his disbelief and gave Adelaide a questioning look. 'Are you satisfied with that pathetic reassurance?'

'Not entirely,' she conceded, 'but do you have any better idea?'

'No, but that doesn't mean that the current one has any merit.'

'It's the only one we have,' Adelaide reminded him as she brushed off his reservations, 'so are we agreed that I'm the one who'll be dressed as a nurse?'

Jennings and Doris nodded, while Matthew simply said, 'No!' loudly and half turned his back on the remainder of them.

'So now that's agreed,' Adelaide grimaced, 'how's it to be set up? All but the bit where I walk up and down the street, that is. I'd prefer to be allowed to sleep here and be with Matthew and Florence overnight, rather than spend the night in some rather dowdy lodging house, so I propose the following. Doris continues to live with us, but on the night before the first morning of this operation I travel to the lodging house with a set of my own clothes. Then in the early hours of that first morning, Father's coach delivers me to the lodging house, where I change into a nurse's uniform.'

'I've got a spare one that should fit you,' Doris offered.

Adelaide nodded. 'Then I walk down to the hospital using the Brick Lane and Whitechapel Road route, inviting Logan to leap out at me. If he doesn't, I spend the day at the hospital and at the end of the day shift the coach brings Doris back here and I walk back to the lodging house. Again assuming that I remain unmolested, I get changed into my ordinary clothes and the coach comes to collect me under the cover of darkness. We repeat that process for every day that Logan doesn't take the bait. Any questions?'

'Yes,' Matthew muttered. 'What do I tell Florence when she's old enough to talk and asks why she doesn't have a mother?'

'Tell her that her father drove her into the arms of a killer by ordering her to stay indoors.'

15

Adelaide took a deep breath and stepped out into the alleyway down the side of the common lodging house into the early morning chill, feeling highly conspicuous in the borrowed gown and cap. When she reached the street, she looked both ways before turning to the right and heading for the bustle and clatter of Brick Lane just a few yards away.

What had seemed like a good idea at the time now seemed like a moment of madness as she waited for some maniac to attack her with a long sharp blade. Suddenly everyone she passed seemed like a potential assassin, and she found herself staring at their hands; if she could see them both and they didn't contain any weapons, then it was safe to pass them by, but she experienced a few heart-stopping moments when she was obliged to step past street traders who had their merchandise heaped on the tops of carts, or in piles to the side of them. Any one of those seemingly innocent bundles could contain a deadly weapon, and she could be struck down in broad daylight by a madman who was a master of disguise and who had already proved how swiftly and silently he could dispose of a nurse.

Adelaide's bravado had lasted until a few hours previously, when Doris had tapped gently on their bedroom door and advised her that it was time for her to dress and that there was tea and toast in the kitchen. Dear, sweet, uncomplaining Doris, who had probably lain awake all night so that she could rouse Adelaide; not that Adelaide had needed any waking, since she'd hardly slept a wink and had spent the night checking her fob watch every ten minutes and trying not to disturb a gently snoring Matthew as she reached out to where it lay on her bedside table.

She hadn't been able to swallow any toast, but had been grateful for the tea. She wasn't sure if she was glad that Matthew had woken when he realised that she was out of bed and had joined her in the spare bedroom that was full of Doris's things, but also contained the cot in which their precious daughter lay. Adelaide had leaned down to give her a kiss, then straightened up and turned to see a silent Matthew standing behind her, tears welling in his eyes. Then the full realisation of what she'd committed herself to had sunk in and it had been perhaps as well that her father's coach had rumbled to a halt at the front door at that very moment and that Matthew had not tried to dissuade her, else her resolve might have cracked.

But it hadn't, and after a few minutes seated in the empty lodging house kitchen here she was, the Aunt Sally in the side show, inviting the attention of a crazed former Guardsman who had already brutally slaughtered three of her colleagues.

There was an extra frisson of fear as she scuttled swiftly past the entrance to the alleyway into which Mary Brennan had been dragged, stabbed to death and abandoned, then she was safely past it. She smiled at the butcher whose face looked up at hers as he placed trays of meat into his display window, then in a few more hasty strides she was into the safety of Whitechapel Road, and the only person who appeared to be following within striking distance of her was an old monk dressed in the sombre grey woollen garment of his order, including the cowl that appeared to be covering his entire head as he mumbled his way along the pavement behind her, his hands tucked into his broad sleeves. It was perhaps as well that he was a man of God, Adelaide reflected, since those wide sleeves could be used to hide an entire arsenal of weapons.

She looked to her right to ensure that there were no carriages coming from the direction of Aldgate, then crossed the busy thoroughfare in order to be on the correct side of the road for the London Hospital. A few yards further down, as she flitted past the imposing facade of a firm of solicitors, she allowed herself a glance behind to her left and noted with rising apprehension that the monk was also crossing Whitechapel Road in order to remain behind her, and if anything he was quickening his pace to walk faster than any monk would normally be expected to do, although his head was still buried deep within his cowl, with his hands firmly hidden inside his sleeves.

The front entrance to the hospital came into sight and Adelaide slipped gratefully into the entrance drive, keeping to the left-hand side in case any coaches came up behind her on an urgent mission to deliver a patient. The third coach to trundle past her looked familiar, and as it drew level the Carlyle family coachman, Williams, raised his whip in a silent greeting. There was a pale face pressed to the window as the coach passed her, and she smiled as she recognised Doris.

Quickening her pace, she caught up with the coach as it slid to a halt, then Williams alighted and walked back down its side in order to open the door for his passenger. He needn't have bothered, since as soon as the horse had come to a halt the door opened from the inside and Doris slid out onto the cobbles.

'You made it here safely, then,' she observed unnecessarily.

Adelaide nodded. 'You're just in time to walk with me down the side and into the nurses' entrance at the rear. I must own that this was the bit I was most dreading, after poor old Edith was attacked back there. Come on — big confident smiles and let's get it over with.'

She allowed herself a nervous glance back up towards Whitechapel Road, where the monk had come to a halt and was staring after her. She shivered and hurried to keep up with Doris as the two of them reached the rear entrance without incident and slipped gratefully into the rear service corridor.

Doris halted in the corridor outside the doors to the Tower Ward, while Adelaide slipped inside, coughing quietly as she kept her head down. Ellen looked up with tired eyes and welcomed her in with a 'Good morning, Doris.' Then she stared in amazement as Doris came through the doors behind Adelaide.

'The disguise obviously fooled you for a second,' Adelaide said, 'so let's hope it has the same effect on the man we're after. Now, to business — anything to report from the night shift?'

'You're going to remain on the day shift?'

'Of course,' Adelaide insisted. 'There's only Doris and me left to represent Miss Nightingale during the day, so off you go home and get some sleep. But make sure you're back in time to let me out of here by six o'clock this evening.'

'Are you going to spend the entire day dressed like that?' Ellen asked.

Adelaide smiled. 'Can you imagine the reaction of our male patients if I stripped down to my undergarments?'

'That's not what I meant,' Ellen chuckled. 'I mean, didn't you bring a change of clothes? If you're not careful, the patients will mistake you for the real thing and demand bedpans and things.'

'I *am* the real thing, up to a point,' Adelaide insisted, 'and even I can carry a bedpan. I'll even undertake to empty it, too, and if there are dressings that need to be changed, I'm well up to that as well.'

Ellen departed with a shake of the head and Adelaide began her working day by reading the Ward Report for the previous night. It wouldn't be long until two more of their patients could be discharged, she estimated, although that would be a decision for her father during his daily ward round.

When he duly appeared on the ward with Matron in tow, he was accompanied by Inspector Jennings, who walked directly down the ward to speak to Adelaide as she sat at the desk. He looked her up and down admiringly before remarking, 'You certainly look the part, as indeed you did as you walked to work.'

'You were watching me?'

'Only briefly. I was one of the customers in the butcher's shop, looking out for you as you passed by.'

'I hope that there were some of your men closer to me than that — presumably including that monk, who was a bit obvious, if you don't mind me saying so.'

'Don't know anything about any monk,' Jennings replied with a look of concern. 'Was he following you?'

'Like a seagull following a fishing boat. But if he wasn't one of yours, who was he?'

'No idea, but I'll get my men to keep an eye on him.'

'So who were they and how come I missed them?'

'I'm glad that you did, since clearly their disguises were effective. Loveday was one of the street hawkers — the one with the plump lady alongside him, who was Mrs Loveday, enjoying a break from her daily housework chores, and young Travener was the boy playing the violin on the corner of Brick Lane, begging for pennies.'

'I thought he might be,' Adelaide said, 'given that his violin playing was so atrocious. But were there only two?'

'There were two more, but you wouldn't have seen them in their shop doorways. Rest assured, you were well covered. But I have to be off — I only called in to reassure myself that you're still in good spirits.'

'I am until I have to take that awful walk in the opposite direction,' Adelaide shuddered. 'Is it all right with you if I leave through the back door in company with Doris? That's the scariest part of the entire journey, if I'm honest with you — the rear exit where poor old Edith was pounced on and knifed. Doris can walk with me to the front entrance and pick up the coach as normal.'

'That's probably in order,' Jennings conceded, 'but no further than that. We'll be watching your return home with the same care as we did your trip down here this morning.'

The day passed without incident until shortly before five o'clock, when the ward doors opened and James Carlyle walked swiftly down between the beds and smiled broadly as he reached the desk. 'Don't tell Matron I'm here,' he whispered.

Adelaide smiled. 'Don't tell me that you're as scared of her as the nurses?'

'Of course not, it's just that she'd insist on dragging me round the beds and prattling on about the quality of nursing they're receiving, when I really just wanted to talk to you. Jennings told me what you're up to and I heartily disapprove, not that my opinion will stop you.'

'Join the club that Matthew recently formed,' Adelaide said. 'But as Jennings also no doubt advised you, he has me well guarded as I walk backwards and forwards between here and the lodging house.'

'That's what he assured me as well,' Carlyle frowned, 'but I chose to underline what a responsibility he'd undertaken by assuring him that if any harm comes to you, I'll perform a sterilisation operation on him without the benefit of any anaesthetic. And I have to say that you just went down in my estimation of you as a mother.'

Adelaide had giggled at the thought of Jennings having his testicles removed without chloroform, but straightened her face to reply to the second remark. 'If ought befalls me, rest assured that there's a perfectly capable old woman at home who can raise her.'

'But Mrs Dunning has other responsibilities of her own, surely?'

'I wasn't referring to her,' Adelaide said, 'and now you'd better go home unless you want to share the coach with Doris. And I hope that you're giving Williams a generous bonus for all the extra work he's doing.'

Adelaide tried to divert her thoughts with ward business as the dreaded hour approached, but well before six o'clock the night shift girls appeared through the doors, giggling quietly to themselves as they left their police escort out in the corridor.

Adelaide parted company with Doris at the coach alongside the front door and walked down the front drive onto Whitechapel Road shortly after six, with the late afternoon sun in her face. Her heart skipped half a beat as she became aware of the same monk leaving by the front door of the solicitors' offices to walk only a few paces behind her, paces that quickened as she increased hers. She risked life and limb to dodge between two heavily laden wagons heading west along the busy thoroughfare and was not surprised to find that the monk appeared to have done likewise and was still only a few paces behind her as she turned, somewhat short of breath, into

Brick Lane and the final few hundred yards of her journey back to the lodging house.

On a whim she pushed open the doors to the butcher's shop, half expecting to find Jennings inside posing as a customer. But she was the only person in there, and as the middle-aged butcher tried to engage her interest in the few remaining tired-looking pieces of meat that lay under his glass counter, she took the opportunity to sneak a glance back outside. There was no sign of the monk, so she ventured back outside and all but ran past the alleyway in which Mary had been murdered until she reached the safety of Finch Street. She looked back before launching herself into the side alley to Number 4 and on the far side of Brick Lane there stood the monk, silently watching her as she turned and headed for the side door and the safety of the communal kitchen.

Then there was what seemed like an interminable wait until Williams arrived with the coach to take her back to Matthew, Florence and home. As she sat at the kitchen table twiddling her thumbs nervously, there was a shuffling noise from down the hallway, and a dowdy women with a crumpled dress stained with something vaguely brown in colour eyed her suspiciously. 'You another o' them nurses?' the woman demanded. 'I'm Ivy Huggins, an' I runs this place. Which one are you, an' which room yer occupyin'?'

'I'm here in place of Lily Becket.'

''Er what got 'erself done in 'cos she left the door open fer 'er fancy man? Make sure yer doesn't make the same mistake, me gel. An' remember that yer both due me a quid at the end o' the week.'

Mercifully, it seemed that Mrs Huggins had only come in search of her spare corkscrew, and having found it at the back of the knife drawer to one side of the stone sink she shuffled back down the hallway, leaving Adelaide alone with her silent thanks to 'whoever' that she didn't actually have to live there permanently. She could now understand why Doris was so appreciative of her temporary accommodation in Curate's House in the grounds of St Dunstan's, and by the time that Williams knocked on the kitchen door to escort her through the darkness of the side alleyway to the coach, Adelaide had quite convinced herself that she was the luckiest woman alive. She'd had an over-indulged childhood courtesy of an adoring father, she was independently wealthy and she lived in a comfortably appointed house with her beautiful daughter, along with what must be the most handsome clergyman in London as her husband.

A husband who was not quite as overjoyed at her return as she had expected. Matthew emerged from the kitchen in a cloud of steam, assured her that he was in the final stages of producing a delicious fish pie unaided and kissed her briefly on the mouth. There was no sound from upstairs, which Adelaide took as an indication that Doris must be upstairs with Florence, and she walked past the open kitchen door on her way to have a wash. She caught sight of something through the door and turned her head sharply in time to see Doris, red-faced and looking guilty, laying cutlery on the dining table. In a sudden, but illogical, fit of jealousy, she glared hard at Doris, then clomped her way heavily up the staircase in search of some cold water and a basin.

As she splashed water on her face, dried her hands on the towel, then dabbed some cologne on her neck, she tried to fight down her suspicions. Matthew and Doris must have known that Adelaide would be returning as soon as darkness had fallen, so why did they react like guilty lovers who'd been caught out? Was Doris's red face the result of being in a steam-filled kitchen, and was Matthew a little cool in his welcome home because he was preoccupied with proving that he could cook? And wasn't she overreacting, putting two and two together to make seven and a half, simply because her nervous system had been badly stretched by the return walk up Brick Lane?

The conversation was subdued over supper and focused mainly on Violet Dunning's experienced opinion that Florence had ceased teething for the time being, until Adelaide dropped her fork on the table in angry exasperation and demanded, 'Is anyone going to ask me how I fared walking back and forth to the lodging house, courting death at each step? Or for that matter, how my day went?'

There was an awkward silence before Matthew replied, 'I obviously knew that you survived this morning's walk, because Doris told me. And you're obviously home in one piece, so I kind of assumed…'

'One should never "assume", Matthew,' Adelaide retorted tartly, 'because it makes an "ass" of "you" and "me". But in answer to your unasked question, it was *very* nerve-racking.'

'I could well imagine that,' Doris replied weakly, 'and hopefully you won't have to do it many more times.'

Adelaide glared across at her with a look little short of murderous. 'You mean that one day in the near future I'll be stabbed in the heart by a lunatic with a bayonet? Because that's the only way this can come to an end, isn't it? Then presumably you'll be only too delighted to remain here, assisting Matthew with Florence's upbringing and pretending to teach him how to cook? At least then you'll have an excuse for the red face when caught out with him in the kitchen!'

Doris's mouth dropped open, then tears appeared in her eyes and she rose from the table with a strangled squawk and rushed from the room. She thundered up the stairs and the sound of her racking sobs could be heard even in the kitchen.

Matthew stared helplessly at Adelaide. 'What on earth prompted that? The poor girl's obviously taken that the wrong way, clearly of the belief that you meant…'

'I know what I meant,' Adelaide hissed back, 'and you didn't misunderstand me — *either* of you!'

Matthew looked stunned. 'I can't bring myself to believe that you'd suspect either of us of … well, of *that*.'

'Well, tell me why I shouldn't,' she retorted. 'I come home to find you both in the kitchen, Doris unable to hide a red face at my arrival, and you can't bring yourself to even ask how I am. Instead you cover your confusion, embarrassment and shame by burbling on about fish!'

Matthew took a few deep breaths to suppress his temper, then turned in his chair to look sideways at his wife and reply coldly, 'I'm sorry if I was too elated at my success in finally being able to cook something for your supper. It's been a long and difficult journey towards domesticity, and all day I've been asking God to preserve you from your own folly. Doris was in tears when she got home, convinced that she'd committed you to a horrible death, and I only thought to ask for her assistance in the kitchen in order to divert her mind from things. If this is what it's going to be like while you're playing the brave heroine for Inspector Jennings, then I'll walk down the street tomorrow morning waving a banner, blowing a trumpet and shouting "If Gerard Logan can hear this, the police have laid this beautiful trap for you, so run away now." Either that or I'll dress up as a nurse and paint a target on my back for his bayonet.'

The sheer absurdity of his suggestion forced Adelaide into a snort of laughter, followed by an attempted protest, then a sob of misery as she collapsed in his arms. 'I'm sorry,' she mumbled eventually as she reached for her handkerchief. 'That walk to and from work must have disarranged my nerves more than I expected. But it *did* look suspicious, you must admit.'

'I'm admitting nothing except responsibility for the fish pie that we've all allowed to get cold,' Matthew said reassuringly as he kissed her nose. 'But while I attempt to re-heat it in the oven, where it'll no doubt dry to the consistency of sawdust, you need to go upstairs and apologise to Doris. And you have to give serious thought to what your chosen mission threatens to do to our marriage.'

'It won't, I promise,' Adelaide assured him as she kissed him. 'We'll give it a week and then I'll reconsider my position.'

16

Adelaide apologised to Doris yet again as they met in the kitchen while the pot was still boiling and before Doris had called Adelaide down for breakfast.

'Please don't feel obliged to keep apologising,' Doris urged her sincerely. 'I quite understand how your nerves must be standing on end with what you've undertaken to do, to save *my* life, remember. I'd probably have jumped to the same wrong conclusion, but I give you my word, on my mother's life, that I don't carry any torch for Matthew. He's a lovely man and you're very lucky to have him, but I could never steal a man from another woman. Now please sit down and eat something. Did you manage to sleep?'

'Very heavily, believe it or not,' Adelaide said. 'Then something woke me up with a start and I thought perhaps it was Florence crying out. But it obviously wasn't and here I am, ready to face that dreadful walk again. But I have something to organise this morning, because I think I know the disguise that my stalker has adopted.'

'You've actually *seen* him?'

'I think so, but I'll let Inspector Jennings deal with him.'

When Williams brought the coach to the door, Adelaide gave him strict instructions to pass a hastily written note to her father, in which she asked him to contact Inspector Jennings as a matter of urgency and arrange for him to apprehend a man dressed as a monk who'd obviously been following her in both directions the previous day. She was aware that Jennings would not get the note until she was, hopefully, safely inside the hospital and she consoled herself, as the monk duly fell in behind her on her morning walk down Brick Lane, that by the time she came out for the return journey he'd be safely under lock and key.

It was therefore with a light heart that, shortly after six that evening, she set off on the return walk from the hospital, with no sign of any monk along Whitechapel Road. She was still grinning with satisfaction as she turned in to Brick Lane and there he was, loitering outside a bookshop, pretending to look at the volumes displayed in the window. She resisted the urge to walk up to him and announce that he'd been spotted and would shortly be in custody and instead just quickened her pace, forcing the monk to scurry along at a thoroughly unholy speed in order to keep up with her.

She heard a shout of protest behind her and looked round with a smirk at the sight of a man dressed as a monk being held up against a wall by someone she'd mistaken for a blind beggar and being questioned regarding his movements by another man dressed like a coach driver. Much lighter at heart she all but skipped the remaining few yards into Finch Street, then back into the lodging house where she changed back into her street clothes and sat at the kitchen table awaiting nightfall, contemplating what might be for supper and hoping that the dreadful Mrs Huggins was lying too drunk in her room to put in an appearance.

The welcome home was indeed a welcome, compared with the previous evening, and Matthew had produced a roast leg of lamb with — or so he was at pains to assure her — no assistance from Doris, who made a point of greeting Adelaide from the staircase, holding a sleeping Florence in her arms.

They were sitting down to tea and mutually agreeing that an early night was called for, when there came a knock on the front door, which Doris insisted on answering. At the first vocal indication that their visitor was Inspector Jennings, Matthew made an excuse and took himself to bed, insisting, 'I'd hate to engage in bloodshed after such a pleasant evening,' leaving Adelaide to offer Jennings a seat as Doris escorted him into the living room.

'You can stop worrying about that monk,' he told her.

'You caught him?'

'We apprehended him, certainly — or at least, two of my men did. But he's genuine, apparently. He's "Brother Brian", a visiting friar from St Dominic's in Hampstead who resides temporarily in lodgings in Aldgate and ministers to Catholic patients in the London Hospital. I'm surprised that you haven't seen him around the place.'

'We often get church ministers wandering in and out, visiting their parishioners,' Adelaide told him, 'but I've never seen a monk around the place. The occasional nun, but never a monk and certainly not that one.'

'Well, he's harmless anyway, so don't worry any more about him.'

'But I still have to worry about Logan, given that he didn't turn out to be the monk?' Adelaide asked.

Jennings nodded. 'I'm afraid so. But you'll be reassured by the speed with which we nabbed the cove this time. Bentino and Jackson were so quick off the mark that I've kept them on for another day or two.'

'Their disguises certainly fooled me,' Adelaide told him. 'Tea?'

'No. Thank you all the same, but the missus is expecting me home. I'll see you tomorrow, although hopefully you won't see me.'

On the third day, Adelaide ignored the monk trotting along almost at her heels, given the reassurance that she'd received from Jennings, and she even managed to lighten what had begun as a terrifying ordeal by seeking to give the monk the slip, since whatever Jennings may have been told about the monk's real business around the East End, he clearly enjoyed following nurses. But try as she may, she couldn't shake him off, and she began to plot a revenge of sorts. She'd wait until he was on one of his ward rounds, then she'd walk in and order him into the de-lousing unit, on suspicion that he was bringing infection into the place.

Around mid-morning, Matron came onto the ward with Carlyle and while he sat on the edge of one of the patient's beds, chatting away about the various prosthetic legs that were available, Adelaide beckoned Matron over to her desk.

'Could you tell me which wards Brother Brian visits?' she asked.

Matron looked puzzled as she asked, 'Who?'

'Brother Brian,' Adelaide repeated as she felt the first nervous flutter in her stomach. 'He's a friar — a sort of monk — who goes around visiting certain patients, and I wanted to meet with him about the possibility of a visit to this ward, to raise morale.'

'My dear,' Matron told her pompously as she drew herself up to her full height, 'I can assure you that no scruffy, flea-ridden itinerant vagabond would be allowed on any of my wards. Priests, vicars, even rabbis — members of recognised ecclesiastical orders — certainly, but equally certainly not those walking pestilences in unwashed rags. You must have been misinformed.'

'Yes, so it would seem,' Adelaide replied as she silently cursed Jennings and his inadequate enquiries. If the man in the hooded robe with the wide sleeves wasn't a genuine monk, then who was he? And — more to the point — why was he following her? She tried to suppress her rising fear by rationalising that if the man inside the disguise really was Logan, then he was taking a long time about attacking her. Surely it was Logan's practice to launch a quick attack out of nowhere, then make himself invisible, whereas "Brother Brian" could not have drawn more attention to himself if he'd been preceded down the street by a brass band.

But rationalise as she might, when the time came for the return walk to the lodging house, Adelaide was trembling with fear and finding it difficult to draw sufficient breath for her rapidly palpitating heart. Almost in a dream she walked the few upwardly sloping yards onto the south side of Whitechapel Road, looking cautiously to the right and left down the overcrowded thoroughfare. There appeared to be no monk in sight, although the street was so busy with pedestrians and wheeled vehicles of all descriptions that she couldn't be certain. 'So far so good,' she muttered under her breath as she struck out in the direction of Brick Lane, crossing to the north side of Whitechapel Road when a rare break in the traffic permitted. Then she saw him and her heart lurched.

He was standing on the far corner of Brick Lane, staring into the window of the haberdashery store that occupied the corner site. As if a monk in holy orders required needle, thread and lace fripperies to sew onto his coarse woollen garment, any more than he needed to visit a city solicitor, as he'd pretended to do on the first afternoon that he'd followed her home. He could only be looking into the window for one reason — to use its reflection in order to keep watch on Adelaide's approach, and *she* could only hope that Jennings's men were as numerous and alert as he'd boasted.

As she turned in to Brick Lane she scanned the busy throng of those who clogged the thoroughfare, hoping to spot one of the disguised police officers and throw herself on their protection. Was one of them the man turning the hurdy-gurdy while pretending to be blind, with a hat on the ground in front of him for alms? Or the street cleaner with his wooden scraper and bucket, ridding the uneven surface of horse dung? Or was Jennings himself back in his original lookout position inside the butcher's shop a few yards up the street on her side of it?

She looked round briefly, then whimpered quietly as she saw the ominous cloaked figure crossing the road after abandoning his pretence of looking in the haberdasher's window. He was now on her side of Brick Lane and closing in rapidly. Adelaide abandoned all attempt at pretence as sheer panic set in and she scurried quickly for the comparative safety of the butcher's shop, where at least she would be out of the advancing clutches of the monk and could arrange for police to be summoned to her assistance to arrest the man who most definitely was *not* "Brother Brian".

Only feet away from the entrance to the butcher's shop was the alleyway in which wagons would unload his fresh provisions and in which unsold off-cuts could be thrown to the packs of dogs that prowled the mean streets. Adelaide was almost past the narrow entrance when a hand shot out from it and pulled her off the street and into the alleyway, then spun her round so that she was facing the busy thoroughfare, with a menacing figure inches away from her, brandishing a bayonet and glaring at her through the narrow slits that were surrounded by healing burn scars. He could dispose of her with one thrust, and since he was blocking the view from the street with his back he could simply walk away once her lifeless form hit the dusty ground. The man opened his mouth in a triumphant grimace, then grunted in surprise as a long arm shot round his throat from behind, while another hand pushed his bayonet downwards and away from any harm to Adelaide.

The two men began struggling violently, as her assailant attempted to raise his bayonet to stab the monk who had interrupted his murderous attack on Adelaide. She watched, fascinated, as her brain finally accepted that the monk had meant her no harm and must have been an additional police watcher of whose existence Jennings had no prior knowledge. Then the monk's cowl fell back in the struggle and Adelaide had never been more glad to see her beloved Matthew, or more fearful for the peril he'd put himself in for her sake.

There was sudden movement from the street entrance to the alleyway and two large men in rough workmen's garb grabbed her would-be assassin and wrestled him to the ground. One of them stamped on his wrist and the bayonet skidded uselessly across the uneven surface. Then the other one smashed into his face with a gnarled fist and Adelaide heard the sickening crunch of breaking bone as the man who was almost certainly Logan gave an animal howl of pain. They hauled him to his feet, one on each arm, and as he stood there, struggling but defenceless, Adelaide was overtaken by a wicked desire generated by the aftermath of the shock she had experienced.

She stepped back, then lunged forward and took careful aim at his groin with her boot, ensuring that the reinforced toe was fully extended. Logan gave another scream and attempted to free his arms, but was subdued by a rain of punches to the head that left him hanging as limp as a scarecrow in a field after heavy rain. The two men dragged him down to the end of the alleyway and into a side alley that led back out onto Whitechapel Road.

Adelaide let out a cry of relief and flung herself into Matthew's arms, as two more men piled into the now deserted alleyway and then looked back, puzzled, at the man and woman locked in each other's arms. They were followed by a red-faced Jennings, who briefly enquired of Adelaide, 'Are you hurt?'

'No,' she gasped, 'thanks to your men. They took him further down the alley and then somewhere off to the right.'

Jennings uttered a foul oath, then ordered his companions to hurry after them. They returned a few moments later, looking utterly defeated, as Adelaide was assuring Matthew for the fourth time that she was unharmed. It was Matthew who enquired whether they would be taking Logan into custody, or to the hospital.

'Neither!' Jennings replied. 'Those weren't my men. The Fenians have got him!'

Adelaide looked up at Matthew with a warm smile. 'You're not very good at either disguises or following people. Perhaps best to stick to preaching. But please don't tell me you've entered holy orders, since I still want you warming my bed. And the sooner you get that disguise off, the better — it doesn't smell too good.'

'No wonder — it's several hundred years old and comes from the Dominican collection in the crypt of St Dunstan's.'

17

The next week proved to be far less hectic and fraught than the previous one. Adelaide handed back the spare nurse's uniform after having it professionally cleaned and was more than happy to turn up on the day shift dressed in her own clothes. There had been several patient discharges and the ward was now down to a mere three, which was all the excuse that she needed to instruct Doris to take the week's leave to which she was entitled.

Then she was reminded that while she was attentive to the welfare of her nurses, there was someone else looking out for her. Late one morning, long after the scheduled ward round, Matron reappeared on the ward carrying a massive flower arrangement in an ornate pot, accompanied by another nurse. She placed the flowers down on Adelaide's desk and before Adelaide could enquire as to the inspiration behind Matron's uncharacteristic act of generosity, she was brusquely advised, 'This is Nurse Pemberton, who'll be taking over your duties. This will leave the entire shift free of Nightingale Nurses, and since there are only three patients on this ward you might wish to contact Miss Nightingale with a view to reducing the staffing levels on the night shift.'

'Have I been dismissed?' Adelaide asked, confused by the sudden change of attitude.

Matron replied with a curt, 'Read the note — I believe that explains everything,' and walked back off the ward, leaving Nurse Pemberton standing politely in front of the desk awaiting the opportunity to slide behind it into Adelaide's seat.

Adelaide extracted the note tucked into the flowers that had been dispatched from a local florist and learned with a contented smile that the order had been placed by Florence Nightingale herself and that the note read:

Thank you for your brave and invaluable work in preserving the life of one of our nurses. The London Hospital no longer requires your supervisory talents, so take two weeks off, then come to tea.

Adelaide's first week off was spent catching up on sleep and reminding herself that for all that she kept antisocial hours, little Florence was a treasure and a delight. Matthew insisted on demonstrating his newly acquired cooking skills, usually with a successful outcome and was more attentive than he had ever been to her every need, particularly once they had retired for the night.

Inspector Jennings had returned, cursing, to Scotland Yard and spent an entire day sending cables to every conceivable law enforcement establishment in the Home Counties, instructing that he be informed of every unexplained and unclaimed male corpse that might be discovered, whatever its condition, in the hope that the Fenians had a policy of leaving their dead where others might find them. This resulted in a depressing procession of corpses being conveyed for the attention of Doctor Carlyle to the basement mortuary of the London Hospital, on occasion being left in malodorous queues on trolleys lining the basement corridor.

At the start of the third week after Adelaide's close encounter with death, Jennings knocked on the door of Curate's House, accompanied by Doris Mooney and in possession of a child's beautifully carved crib. Adelaide instinctively threw her arms around Doris with loving endearments and invited them both in for tea and almond cake. They followed her into the kitchen, where Matthew stood with his arms immersed in a flour bowl almost to his elbow.

'Look at this beautiful crib!' Adelaide called out to him, and Matthew looked first at the crib, then up at Jennings and his mouth set in a smirk.

'Let me guess — they threw you off the force for losing Logan to the Fenians and you've taken to your former trade as a wood carver. You're better at that than you were at protecting my wife from a homicidal lunatic, to judge by that crib — it's not half bad.'

'It's from Doris,' Adelaide corrected him.

'I met Miss Mooney on the driveway, where she was staggering towards your house with it,' Jennings explained, and Doris added the remaining detail.

'My older brother carved it for me. He's a skilled craftsman, and I wanted to thank you in the most appropriate way I knew for saving my life — both of you.'

'Not me,' Matthew conceded modestly. 'That was Adelaide.'

'True,' Adelaide said as she walked round the table and kissed Matthew on the lips, 'but it took Matthew to save *my* life.'

'Thank you for rubbing it in,' Jennings said, 'but I'm here in connection with that. We believe that the Fenians may finally have got round to leaving Logan's body for collection, and since Adelaide was the last one to see him alive, we'd be grateful if you'd come down and identify him for us.'

'By "we", do you mean my father?' Adelaide asked.

Jennings nodded. 'I've sent him a few stray corpses in the past few weeks, I'm afraid, so he currently has the same regard for me as he would have for an outbreak of the Plague, but this time he thinks we may have the right one. In fact, he's damned near certain, but we need a formal identification for legal purposes and his wife — or is it his widow? — told us to go and jump in the Thames. In either case the body's in a bit of a mess, I'm afraid.'

The smell inside the mortuary was all too familiar to Adelaide and Jennings, but instantly nauseating to Matthew, who gagged, then hastily pulled out a pocket handkerchief and pressed it hard against his nose and mouth. 'How long has *that* been dead?' he asked in a muffled voice as he nodded towards the long lump on the table.

'About a week, I'd estimate,' Carlyle said as he reached into a drawer for a jar of green cream that smelt strongly of peppermint, which he tossed towards Matthew with an instruction to spread some across his top lip.

Matthew did as suggested and nearly choked on the fumes. Carlyle invited them closer to the table, and while Matthew hung back with a shudder, Adelaide and Jennings took up positions on either side of the grisly male cadaver.

'Remind us all of its provenance?' Carlyle requested with a nod in Jennings's direction, and the inspector duly obliged.

'Nailed to the front door of an abandoned shop in Limehouse, a few streets away from the Fenian Barracks. I think it was meant as a warning to all those who irritate the Brotherhood in some way, and it was a very brave local resident who eventually sent an anonymous note to the local jail.'

'Why didn't the police find it during a routine patrol?' Matthew demanded.

Jennings smiled grimly. 'There's no such thing as a routine patrol in Limehouse — I thought you learned that while rescuing those parish children two years ago. The police only go in there in groups of half a dozen or more, and when they do they are frequently accompanied by armed soldiers.'

'When you say "nailed to the door",' Matthew asked fearfully, 'do you mean crucified?'

Carlyle shook his head. 'Not while alive, anyway. There'd be more obvious bloodstains around the nail marks had that been the case. But don't tell me that you feel some sympathy for the man who tried to kill your wife and my daughter?'

'Of course not, but… Well, I mean, the sheer brutality of it!'

'The Fenian Brotherhood fall somewhat behind the Salvation Army in their charitable response to those who get on the wrong side of them,' Jennings told him. 'Now, Doctor, what makes you think it's Logan? And how can you tell, given the fact that someone seriously rearranged his face?'

'He was brutally beaten, certainly,' Carlyle told the company. 'I lost count of the number of broken bones, and I would imagine that the cause of death was the rupture of several internal organs such as the spleen. But the bruising was only superficial and didn't conceal the evidence of burn marks around the eyes.'

'The entire face looks burned,' Matthew argued.

Carlyle nodded. 'Only to the inexperienced eye. What you're looking at there is decomposition — the deep red, greenish and occasional yellow bits. Allowing for the fact that it develops more quickly at the site of a contusion such as a bruise, and comparing it with the lesser indications of putrescence elsewhere on the torso, enables me to give you the time estimate of a week since death.'

'So how can you be sure that the man was burned around the eyes?' Adelaide asked. 'The scarring appeared deep for the brief second in which I saw it, but it seems to have got lost in all the putrescence.'

Her father smiled and tapped the side of his nose. 'Not if you know what you're looking for. It was all too easy to pull the bruised skin away, given the state it was in, and beneath it was the remaining evidence of burns that went very deep. There's scarring still visible and striations on the cheek bones, entirely consistent with whoever this was having sustained deep burns to the area around the eyes at some stage prior to death. That's consistent with what I recall of Captain Logan, but that's just about all.'

'Height?' Jennings asked hopefully.

Carlyle nodded. 'Again, probably consistent with the man Logan. The body bulk had begun to shrink through the decomposition effect, but I took great care in measuring the skeleton. This man would have been six feet and one inch tall when alive, and although I never saw him standing up I believe that there were references to whoever killed those three nurses having been a tall man.'

'That's certainly how I recall the man who attacked me,' Adelaide shuddered, 'but is there nothing else you can tell us?'

Her father sighed. 'Look at the state of what's left, for heaven's sake. You, above all people, Adelaide, must appreciate the enormity of identifying someone that none of us really saw without bandages covering his entire face. And the injuries inflicted on him before he died only made matters worse. He even had a ruptured testicle, would you believe?'

Adelaide burst out laughing, then nodded gleefully. 'That's almost certainly Logan, then.'

'How can you possibly tell that?' Carlyle asked and it was Matthew's turn to laugh.

'There are things you clearly have yet to learn about the sweet little girl that you raised, James.'

EPILOGUE

John Sweeney had married Lila Drake two hours earlier in the lovely old church of St Peter-in-Thanet, on the outskirts of Lila's hometown of Broadstairs. By special licence and at John's personal request, Matthew had been proud to conduct the ceremony and was still dressed in his stole and other vestments as they stood on the rear terrace that overlooked the cottage garden that went with the delightful thatched house that Lila had called home. Now she was in the first day of her life as the wife of a captain in the Coldstream Guards.

'This makes a pleasant change from the dirty narrow streets of the East End,' Matthew commented as he gazed wistfully down at a row of delphiniums that were just past their best now that October was nearly upon them.

Adelaide looked at him in faint horror. 'I hope that you're not thinking of seeking a parish like this one, miles from anywhere and so distant from where we were both brought up?' she asked.

Matthew sighed. 'We had no choice as to where we were born and raised. And is it such a blessing, to be living our lives amongst all that crime and squalor? Here in the country we can more clearly hear the word of God.'

'Perhaps *you* can, but all I heard when we woke up in that hotel room this morning was an entire wood full of noisy crows.'

'So you'd rather hear the rumble of carriages and buses and smell the horse dung?' Matthew countered. 'And I'm bound to observe that you didn't deny the crime and squalor — the world of Inspector Jennings and his thugs. The permanent procession of dead bodies in and out of your father's mortuary.'

'Leave my father out of this. Thanks to him I have a career in medicine.'

'You have a career trotting around the country at the whim of Florence Nightingale, you mean. How long before she sends you off to Liverpool, or Manchester, or another of those dreadful smoky dumps?'

'She won't for the time being, which is perhaps as well in the circumstances. My next set of duties will be inside the Middlesex Hospital, which is only a bus ride north of us, in Mortimer Street. Doris Mooney was transferred there when she came back after her holiday, and she sent me a letter telling me that the Nightingale Nurses deployed there have become a little slack in their observance of the Pledge, given the distractions of the West End. I alerted Florence and she's asked me to prepare myself to start duties there in a week or two.'

'You *were* going to get round to telling me before you simply walked out one morning, I take it?'

'Of course. Although I'd feel happier about doing so if I didn't think that you'd get yourself into more trouble during the days when I'm away.'

'You mean trouble such as saving you from a lunatic armed with a bayonet?'

It was Adelaide's turn to sigh heavily. 'Are you ever going to stop reminding me of that? You were there at the right moment, that's all.'

'And a good job I was, because Jennings and his oafs would have been too late. They weren't even there in time to stop the Fenians from spiriting Logan away. Jennings was livid that he couldn't take the credit, and he even had to hand over a prisoner in order to get the Fenian boss to admit that Logan was dead.'

Matthew was still resentful of the fact that Jennings had agreed to drop the assault charge against Finnegan — arising from his attack on Matthew in the street across from The Shamrock — in exchange for the Fenians writing to the leading London newspapers to boast of having exacted their own justice on the man who'd planted the bomb in the Tower, then overstepped the mark by murdering three innocent nurses.

'Well, it worked out all right at the end of the day, didn't it?' Adelaide argued. 'Jennings got the credit for tracking down Logan and handing him over for instant justice rather than risk a jury acquitting him because of the flimsy evidence, and the public were reassured that Jack the Ripper hadn't returned.'

'It worked out well for Jennings, certainly,' Matthew conceded grumpily, 'but you nearly got killed, and I finished up getting a thumping for nothing.'

'Not necessarily for nothing,' Adelaide said. 'At least you learned that there are places where it's not healthy to go preaching. So perhaps you might want to divest yourself of your religious outfit and let us go back in there like a normal couple with a family of our own.'

'Can Florrie be described as a family all by herself?' Matthew asked. 'Isn't that rather a heavy responsibility to impose on such a lovely, vulnerable child of God?'

'She's called Florence, for the umpteenth time. Let's hope you get the next one right.'

'What next one?' Matthew asked.

'You clearly weren't listening, as usual, when I referred earlier to the fact that my next working location will be a bus ride away in Mortimer Street. If you recall, I said that it was perhaps as well in the circumstances. Well, those circumstances include the current state of my womb.'

'I wonder if it'll be a boy or a girl,' Matthew mused out loud, a broad smile on his face.

'If it's a boy, I want to call him James, after his grandfather,' Adelaide insisted firmly. 'And woe betide you if you start calling him "Jimmy". Then there might not be any more children.'

'An idle threat,' Matthew smirked. 'You enjoy it as much as I do.'

'That's not exactly what I meant,' Adelaide replied sweetly. 'You've seen what I can do with the toe of my boot.'

A NOTE TO THE READER

Dear Reader,

Thank you for following the lives of Matthew, Adelaide and James through this fourth novel in the 'Carlyle and West' series. I enjoyed researching it as much as I did writing it, since there is so much rich and detailed information available regarding life in late Victorian London, and as usual I was able to give my characters a realistic background against which to live out their lives.

One of the most dominant figures in the backdrop to this novel is of course the truly remarkable Florence Nightingale, a woman well ahead of her time and a perfect role model for the feisty and self-liberated Adelaide. Like Adelaide, Florence Nightingale was raised to upper-middle-class privilege, and like Adelaide she kicked hard against the expectation that she would 'marry well' and be valued in accordance with the status of her spouse. Instead, she heard the call of God when she opted to study nursing and learned, through influential social contacts, of the conditions being endured by English troops in the Crimea.

She is these days best remembered for what she did next — creating and managing, with a stern insistence upon hygiene and record-keeping, the hospital at Scutari that become a benchmark for nursing standards. Lionised and feted as 'The Lady with the Lamp', she returned to England when the war was over and used her fame and influence to establish the 'Nightingale Training School' for nurses at St Thomas's Hospital in South London. The rest of her life was devoted to the profession of nursing, and in addition to sending her trained nurses out like medical missionaries around the country, she wrote what became the standard training textbook of its time, *Notes on Nursing*.

It was only too easy to appoint, as her representative out in the field, my heroine Adelaide, with her almost identical ambition to see women established in professional life. Florence would, by 1895, have been in her mid-seventies and dogged by poor health, so the availability of someone as reliable, loyal and resolutely determined as Adelaide would have been seen by Florence as another sign from God that she had been correct in her life choices. Florence eventually died in 1910, by which time she was as much an icon of English life as her contemporary, Queen Victoria, although not so remote. But it was in keeping with the woman she was that Florence's family declined the offer of burial in Westminster Abbey and her final resting place is in a modest churchyard in Hampshire.

The other strong background influence in this novel is that of 'The Fenian Brotherhood'. I did not exaggerate the disruption to everyday life that was caused by this determined, and frequently violent, pressure group dedicated to Irish Home Rule, and 'the Irish Question' dominated Parliamentary life for most of the late Victorian period. By 1895 the Fenians already had a deplorable reputation for explosive outrages involving Establishment symbols such as army barracks, railway stations, town halls, police stations, the House of Commons and the Tower of London.

It was therefore not unreasonable for me to credit them with one more, inside the Officers' Mess of the Coldstream Guards stationed on ceremonial guard duties inside the Waterloo Barracks of the Tower. Nor was 'the Fenian Barracks' a wild fictional exaggeration on my part; it really existed, exactly where I placed it, in a narrow enclave of terraced houses along

Fern and Rook Streets in Poplar. Entry was all but denied to law enforcement representatives, and I based my description of it on the respected 1891 survey of East London by social historian Charles Booth, who noted that it sent more police to hospital than any other block in London. A fitting location for a low 'Irish pub' whose activities included the corruption of English Army officers who could be exploited in the Irish cause.

Finally, the ease with which the inhabitants of the East End could be terrified by the mere suggestion of the return of the beast who had stalked their streets less than a decade earlier under the assumed name of 'Jack the Ripper'. Even today, his identity remains one of the greatest unsolved crime mysteries of English history, due to the failure of the Metropolitan Police to capture or even name him. Whoever he was, he is long dead now, but a mere seven years after his last known victim slid to the pavement with her throat slit, it was possible to whip up a frenzy of renewed terror by suggesting that his was the hand behind every random murder of a woman, of which the East End of London regrettably had no shortage in those precarious times.

Obviously my main characters are fictitious, and I hope that you've enjoyed following their intertwined lives in the pages of this and the preceding three novels in the series. I would welcome any feedback and support that you, the reader, can supply. You can, of course, write a review on **Amazon** or **Goodreads** or you can contact me online via my Facebook page: **DavidFieldAuthor**. I'm more than happy to respond to observations, reviews, questions, or anything else that occurs to you, or to join in any 'thread' that you care to begin. I look forward to getting to know you better online.

David

Sapere Books is an exciting new publisher of brilliant fiction and popular history.

To find out more about our latest releases and our monthly bargain books visit our website:
saperebooks.com

Printed in Great Britain
by Amazon

81226716R00122